Hanford Lennox Gordon

Legends of the Northwest

Hanford Lennox Gordon

Legends of the Northwest

ISBN/EAN: 9783337392543

Printed in Europe, USA, Canada, Australia, Japan

Cover: Foto ©Andreas Hilbeck / pixelio.de

More available books at **www.hansebooks.com**

LEGENDS OF THE NORTHWEST.

BY

H. L. GORDON,

Author of "Pauline."

CONTAINING

PRELUDE—THE MISSISSIPPI.

THE FEAST OF THE VIRGINS,
A LEGEND OF THE DAKOTAS.

WINONA,
A LEGEND OF THE DAKOTAS.

THE LEGEND OF THE FALLS,
A LEGEND OF THE DAKOTAS.

THE SEA GULL,
THE OJIBWA LEGEND OF THE PICTURED ROCKS OF LAKE SUPERIOR.

MINNETONKA.

ST. PAUL, MINN.
THE ST. PAUL BOOK AND STATIONERY CO.

1881.

PREFACE.

I have for several years devoted many of my leisure hours to the study of the language, history, traditions, customs and superstitions of the Dakotas. These Indians are now commonly called the "Sioux".—a name given them by the early French traders and *voyageurs*. "Dakota," signifies *alliance* or *confederation*. Many separate bands, all having a common origin and speaking a common tongue, were united under this name. See "*Tah-Koo Wah-Kan*," or "*The Gospel Among the Dakotas*," by Stephen R. Riggs, pp. 1 to 6 inc.

They were, but yesterday, the occupants and owners of the fair forests and fertile prairies of Minnesota,—a brave, hospitable and generous people,—barbarians, indeed, but noble in their barbarism. They may be fitly called the Iroquois of the West. In form and features, in language and traditions, they are distinct from all other Indian tribes. When first visited by white men, and for many years afterwards, the Falls of St. Anthony (by them called the Ha-Ha) was the center of their country. They cultivated tobacco, and hunted the elk, the beaver and the bison. They were open-hearted, truthful and brave. In their wars with other tribes they seldom slew women or children, and rarely sacrificed the lives of their prisoners.

For many years their chiefs and head men successfully resisted the attempts to introduce spirituous liquors among them. More than a century ago an English trader was killed at Mendota, because he persisted, after repeated warnings by the chiefs, in dealing out *mini wakan* (Devilwater) to the Dakota braves.

With open arms and generous hospitality they welcomed the first white men to their land; and were ever faithful in their friendship, till years of wrong and robbery, and want and insult, drove them to desperation and to war. They were barbarians, and their warfare was barbarous, but not more barbarous than the warfare of our Saxon and Celtic ancestors. They were ignorant and superstitious, but their condition closely resembled the condition of our British forefathers at the beginning of the Christian era. Macaulay says of Britain, "Her inhabitants, when first they became known to the Tyrian mariners, were litttle superior to the natives of the Sandwich Islands." And again, "While the German princes who reigned at Paris, Toledo, Arles and Ravenna listened with reverence to the instructions of Bishops, adored the relics of martyrs, and took part eagerly in disputes touching the Nicene theology, the rulers of Wessex and Mercia were still performing savage rites in the temples of Thor and Woden."

The day of the Dakotas is done. The degenerate remnants of that once powerful and warlike people still linger around the forts and agencies of the Northwest, or chase the caribou and the bison on the banks of the Sascatchewan, but the Dakotas of old are no more. The brilliant defeat of Custer, by Sitting Bull and his braves, was their last grand rally against the resistless march of the sons of the Saxons and the Celts. The plow-shares of a superior race are fast leveling the sacred mounds of their dead. But yesterday, the shores of our lakes, and our rivers, were dotted with their tepees. Their light canoes glided over our waters, and their hunters chased the deer and the buffalo on the sites of our cities. To-day, they are not. Let us do justice to their memory, for there was much that was noble in their natures.

In the following Dakota Legends I have endeavored to faithfully represent many of the customs and superstitions, and some of the traditions, of that people. I have taken very little "poetic license" with their traditions; none, whatever, with their customs and superstitions. In my studies for these Legends I have been greatly aided by Rev. S. R. Riggs, author of the Grammar and Dictionary of the Dakota language, "Tâh-Koo Wah-Kàn," &c., and for many years a missionary among the Dakotas. He has patiently answered my numerous inquiries and given me valuable information. I am also indebted to Gen. H. H. Sibley, one of the earliest American traders among them, and to Rev. S. W. Pond, of Shakopee, one of the first Protestant missionaries to these people, and himself the author of poetical versions of some of their principal legends; to Mrs. Eastman's "Dacotah," and last, but not least, to the Rev. E. D. Neill, whose admirable "History of Minnesota" so fully and faithfully presents almost all that is known of the history, traditions, customs, manners and superstitions of the Dakotas.

In *Winona* I have "tried my hand" on Hexameter verse. With what success, I leave to those who are better able to judge than I. If I have failed, I have but added another failure to the numerous vain attempts to naturalize Hexameter verse in the English language.

The Earl of Derby, in the preface to his translation of the Iliad, calls it "That 'pestilent heresy' of the so-called English Hexameter; a metre wholly repugnant to the genius of our language; which can only be pressed into the service by a violation of every rule of prosody." Lord Kames, in his "Elements of Criticism," says, "Many attempts have been made to introduce Hexameter verse into the living languages, but without success. The English language, I am inclined to think, is not susceptible of this melody, and my reasons are these: First, the polysyllables in Latin and Greek are finely diversified by long and short syllables, a circumstance that qualifies them for the melody of Hexameter verse: ours are extremely ill qualified for that service, because they super-abound in short syllables. Secondly, the bulk of our monosyllables are arbitrary with regard to length, which is an unlucky circumstance in Hexameter. *   *   * In Latin and Greek Hexameter invariable sounds direct and ascertain the melody. English Hexameter would be destitute of melody, unless by artful pronunciation; because of necessity the bulk of its sounds must be arbitrary. The pronunciation is easy in a simple movement of alternate long and short syllables; but would be perplexing and unpleasant in the diversified movement of Hexameter verse."

Beautiful as is the _Evangeline_ of Longfellow, his Hexameter lines are sometimes hard to scan, and often grate harshly on the ear. He is frequently forced to divide a word by the central or pivotal pause of the line, and sometimes to make a pause in the sense where the rhythm forbids it. Take for example some of the opening lines of _Evangeline:_

> "This is the forest prime||val. The murmuring pines and the hemlocks,
>   Bearded with moss, and in gar||ments green, indistinct in the twilight.
> Loud from its rocky cav||erns, the deep-voiced neighboring ocean
>   Speaks, and in accents discon||solate answers the wail of the forest.
> Lay in the fruitful val||ley. Vast meadows stretched to the eastward."

Again, in order to comply with the Greek and Latin rule of beginning each line with a _long_ syllable, he is compelled to emphasize words contrary to the sense. Examples:

> _In_ the Acadian land, on the shores of the Basin of Minas.
> _Some_what apart from the vil||lage, and nearer the Basin of Minas.
> _But_ a celestial bright||ness—a more etherial beauty.
> _And_ the retreating sun the sign of the scorpion enters.
> _In_-doors, warmed by the wide-||mouthed fireplace idly the farmer,
> _Four_ times the sun had ris||en and set; and now on the fifth day,

"Greek and Latin Hexameter lines, as to time, are all of the same length, being equivalent to the time taken in pronouncing twelve long syllables, or twenty-four short ones. An Hexameter line may consist of seventeen syllables, and when regular and not Spondiac, it never has fewer than thirteen: whence it follows that where the syllables are many, the plurality must be short; where few, the plurality must be long.

This line is susceptible of much variety as to the succession of long and short syllables. It is however subject to laws that confine its variety within certain limits. * * *

1st. The line must always commence with a *long* syllable, and close with two long preceded by two short.

2d. More than two short syllables can never be found together, nor *fewer* than two.

3d. Two long syllables which have been preceded by two short can not also be followed by two short.

These few rules fulfill all the conditions of an Hexameter line with relation to order of arrangement."—*Lord Kames*, "*Elements of Criticism*."

One who attempts to write English Hexameter, under the Greek and Latin rules, will speedily be made aware that the English language "superabounds in short syllables." Why then should we rigidly adhere to rules repugnant to the genius of our language, if they can be modified so as to adapt the sonorous Hexameter to the structure of our mother-tongue? Can they be so modified? I have attempted it. I venture to change them as follows:

1st. By beginning each line with a *short* syllable instead of a long one. And it will be seen that I often begin a line with two short syllables.

2d. By often using one short syllable unaccompanied by another.

3d. I have increased the average number of syllables in the line to better adapt it to our super-abundance of short syllables.

4th. In *Winona* I have introduced a rhyme at the pivotal pause of the line, not because my Hexameter requires it, but because I think it increases the melody, and more emphatically marks the central pause.

I am not quite sure that, in a long poem, the rhyme is not detrimental. That depends greatly, however, upon the skill with which it is handled. Surely the same Hexameter can be written as smoothly and more vigorously without rhyme. Rhyme adds greatly to the labor of composition; it rarely assists, but often hinders, the expression of the sense which the author would convey. At times I have been on the point of abandoning it in despair, but after having been under the hammer and the file, at intervals, for the last four years, *Winona* is at last *done*, if not finished.

It will be observed that I have slightly changed the length and the rhythm of the old Hexameter line; but it is still Hexameter. and, I think, improved. I am not afraid of intelligent criticism. I invoke it. and will endeavor to profit by it in the future as in the past.

The reception of my "*Pauline*," at home and abroad. has been so flattering that I have been encouraged to attempt something better. That was my first real effort and full of crudities; but ·if the Legends are received by our best critics as well as "*Pauline*" was received. I shall be well pleased with my efforts.

After much thought I have decided to publish the first edition of my *Legends* here at home.

1st. Because they pertain particularly to the lakes and rivers, to the fair forests and fertile fields of our own Minnesota; and ought to be appreciated here if anywhere.

2d. Because many of our people are competent to judge whether my representations of Dakota customs, life, traditions and superstitions are correct or not; and, at the same time. the reading public of the North-west is as intelligent and discriminating as that of any other portion of our country. If these *Legends* be appreciated and approved by our own people, who are familiar with the scenery described. and more or less, with the customs, traditions and superstitions of the Dakotas; and if, beyond that, these poems shall stand the test of candid criticism. I may give them a wider publication.

H. L. GORDON.

MINNEAPOLIS, June 1, 1881.

PRELUDE.

THE MISSISSIPPI.

Onward rolls the Royal River, proudly sweeping to the sea,
Dark and deep and grand, forever wrapt in myth and mystery.
Lo he laughs along the highlands, leaping o'er the granite walls;
Lo he sleeps among the islands, where the loon her lover calls.
Still like some huge monster winding downward through the prairied plains,
Seeking rest but never finding, till the tropic gulf he gains.
In his mighty arms he claspeth now an empire broad and grand;
In his left hand lo he graspeth leagues of fen and forest land;
In his right, the mighty mountains, hoary with eternal snow,
Where a thousand foaming fountains singing seek the plains below.

Fields of corn and feet of cities lo the mighty river laves,
Where the Saxon sings his ditties o'er the swarthy warriors' graves.

Aye, before the birth of Moses—ere the Pyramids were piled—
All his banks were red with roses from the sea to nor'lands wild,
And from forest, fen and meadows, in the deserts of the north,
Elk and bison stalked like shadows, and the tawny tribes came forth;
Deeds of death and deeds of daring on his leafy banks were done—
Women loved and men went warring—ere the siege of Troy begun.
Where his wayward waters thundered, roaring o'er the rocky walls,
Dusky hunters sat and wondered, listening to the spirits' calls.
"Ha-ha!"[76] cried the warrior greeting from afar the cataract's roar;
"Ha-ha!" rolled the answer, beating down the rock-ribbed leagues of shore.
Now, alas, the bow and quiver and the dusky braves have fled,
And the sullen, shackled river drives the droning mills instead.

Where the war-whoop rose, and, after, women wailed their warriors slain,
List the Saxon's silvery laughter, and his humming hives of gain.
Swiftly sped the tawny runner o'er the pathless prairies then,
Now the iron-reindeer sooner carries weal or woe to men.
On thy bosom, Royal River, silent sped the birch canoe,
Bearing brave with bow and quiver, on his way to war or woo;
Now with flaunting flags and streamers—mighty monsters of the deep—
Lo the puffing, panting steamers, through thy foaming waters sweep;
And behold the grain-fields golden, where the bison grazed of eld;
See the fanes of forests olden by the ruthless Saxon felled,—
Pluméd pines that spread their shadows ere Columbus spread his sails,
Firs that fringed the mossy meadows ere the Mayflower braved the gales,
Iron oaks that nourished bruin while the Vikings roamed the main,
Crashing fall in broken ruin for the greedy marts of gain.

Still forever and forever rolls the restless river on,
Slumbering oft but ceasing never, while the circling centuries run.

In his palm the lakelet lingers, in his hair the brooklets hide,
Grasped within his thousand fingers lies a continent fair and wide,—
Yea, a mighty empire swarming with its millions like the bees,
Delving, drudging, striving, storming, all their lives, for golden ease.

Still, methinks, the dusky shadows of the days that are no more
Stalk around the lakes and meadows, haunting oft the wonted shore,—
Hunters from the land of spirits seek the bison and the deer,
Where the Saxon now inherits golden field and silver mere;
And beside the mound where burried lies the dark-eyed maid he loves,
Some tall warrior, wan and wearied, in the misty moonlight moves.
See—he stands erect and lingers—stoic still, but loth to go—
Clutching in his tawny fingers feathered shaft and polished bow.
Never wail or moan he utters and no tear is on his face,
But 'a warrior's curse he mutters on the crafty Saxon race.

O thou dark, mysterious River, speak and tell thy tales to me;
Seal not up thy lips forever—veiled in mist and mystery.
I will sit and lowly listen at the phantom-haunted falls,
Where thy waters foam and glisten o'er the rugged, rocky walls.
Till some spirit of the olden, mystic, weird, romantic days
Shall emerge and pour her golden tales and legends through my lays.
Then again the elk and bison on thy grassy banks shall feed,
And along the low horizon shall the pluméd hunter speed;
Then again on lake and river shall the silent birch canoe
Bear the brave with bow and quiver on his way to war or woo:
Then the beaver on the meadow shall rebuild his broken wall,
And the wolf shall chase his shadow and his mate the panther call.
From the prairies and the regions where the pine-plumed forest grows
Shall arise the tawny legions with their lances and their bows;
And again the shouts of battle shall resound along the plain,
Bows shall twang and quivers rattle, women wail their warriors slain.

ICE SCENE—SCALES OF ST. ANTHONY.

THE FEAST OF THE VIRGINS.[1]

A LEGEND OF THE DAKOTAS.

(In pronouncing Dakota words give "a" the sound of "ah"—"e" the sound of "a"—
"i" the sound of "e" and "u" the sound of "oo," sound "ee" as in English. The numerals, 1, 2, etc., refer to explanatory notes in the appendix.)

THE GAME OF BALL.[2]

Clear was the sky as a silver shield;
The bright sun blazed on the frozen field.
On ice-bound river and white-robed prairie
The diamonds gleamed in the flame of noon:
But cold and keen were the breezes airy
Wa-zí-ya[3] blew from his icy throne.

On the solid ice of the silent river
The bounds are marked, and a splendid prize.
A robe of black-fox lined with beaver—
Is hung in view of the eager eyes;
And fifty merry Dakota maidens,
The fairest-moulded of woman kind,
Are gathered in groups on the level ice.
They look on the robe and its beauty gladdens,
And maddens their hearts for the splendid prize.
Lo the rounded ankles and raven hair
That floats at will on the wanton wind,
And the round brown arms to the breezes bare.

And breasts like the mounds where the waters meet,[1]
And feet as fleet as the red deer's feet,
And faces that glow like the full, round moon
When she laughs in the luminous skies of June.

The leaders are chosen and swiftly divide
The opposing parties on either side.
Wiwâstè[5] is chief of a nimble band,
The star-eyed daughter of Little Crow;[6]
And the leader chosen to hold command
Of the band adverse is a haughty foe—
The dusky, impetuous Hârpstinà,[7]
The queenly cousin of Wapasa.[8]

Kapóza's chief and his tawny hunters
Are gathered to witness the queenly game.
The ball is thrown and a bat encounters,
And away it flies with a loud acclaim.
Swift are the maidens that follow after,
And swiftly it flies for the farther bound;
And long and loud are the peals of laughter,
As some fair runner is flung to ground;
While backward and forward. and to and fro,
The maidens contend on the trampled snow.
With loud "Ihó!—Itó!—Ihó!"[9]
And waving the beautiful prize anon.
The dusky warriors cheer them on.
And often the limits are almost passed,
As the swift ball flies and returns.   At last
It leaps the line at a single bound
From the fair Wiwâstè's sturdy stroke,

Like a fawn that flies from the baying hound.
Wild were the shouts, and they rolled and broke
On the beetling bluffs and the hills profound,
An echoing, jubilant sea of sound.
Wakâwa, the chief, and the loud acclaim
Announced the end of the well-fought game,
And the fair Wiwâstè was victor crowned.

Dark was the visage of Hârpstinà
When the robe was laid at her rival's feet,
And merry maidens and warriors saw
Her flashing eyes and her look of hate,
As she turned to Wakâwa, the chief, and said:—
"The game was mine were it fairly played.
I was stunned by a blow on my bended head,
As I snatched the ball from slippery ground
Not half a fling from Wiwâstè's bound.
And the cheat—behold her! for there she stands
With the prize that is mine in her treacherous hands.
The fawn may fly, but the wolf is fleet;
The fox creeps sly on Magâ's [m] retreat;
And a woman's revenge—it is swift and sweet."
She turned to her lodge, but a roar of laughter
And merry mockery followed after.
Little they heeded the words she said,
Little they cared for her haughty tread,
For maidens and warriors and chieftain knew
That her lips were false and her charge untrue.

Wiwâstè, the fairest Dakota maiden,
The sweet-faced daughter of Little Crow,

To her teepee turned with her trophy laden—
The black robe trailing the virgin snow.
Beloved was she by her princely father,
Beloved was she by the young and old,
By merry maidens and many a mother,
And many a warrior bronzed and bold.
For her face was as fair as a beautiful dream,
And her voice like the song of the mountain stream;
And her eyes like the stars when they glow and gleam
Through the somber pines of the nor'land wold,
When the winds of winter are keen and cold.

Mah-pi-ya Dú-ta, [12] the tall Red Cloud,
A hunter swift and a warrior proud,
With many a scar and many a feather,
Was a suitor bold and a lover fond.
Long had he courted Wiwâstè's father,
Long had he sued for the maiden's hand.
Aye, brave and proud was the tall Red Cloud,
A peerless son of a giant race,
And the eyes of the panther were set in his face.
He strode like a stag, and he stood like a pine;
Ten feathers he wore of the great Warmdeè; [13]
With crimsoned quills of the porcupine
His leggins were worked to his brawny knee.   .
The bow he bent was a giant's bow;
The swift red elk could he overtake,
And the necklace that girdled his brawny neck
Was the polished claws of the great Mató [14]
He grappled and slew in the northern snow.

Wiwâstè looked on the warrior tall;
She saw he was brawny and brave and great,
But the eyes of the panther she could but hate,
And a brave Hóhé[15] loved she better than all.
Loved was Mahpíya by Hârpstinà.
But the warrior she never could charm or draw;
And bitter indeed was her secret hate
For the maiden she reckoned so fortunate.

HEYÓKA WACÍPEE[16]—THE GIANT'S DANCE.

The night-sun[17] sails in his gold canoe,
The spirits[18] walk in the realms of air
With their glowing faces and flaming hair,
And the shrill, chill winds o'er the prairies blow.
In the Tee[19] of the Council the Virgins light
The Virgin-fire[20] for the feast to-night;
For the Sons of Heyóka will celebrate
The sacred dance to the giant great.
The kettle boils on the blazing fire,
And the flesh is done to the chief's desire.
With his stoic face to the sacred East,[21]
He takes his seat at the Giant's Feast.

For the feast of Heyóka[22] the braves are dressed
With crowns from the bark of the white-birch trees,
And new skin leggins that reach the knees;
With robes of the bison and swarthy bear,
And eagle-plumes in their coal-black hair,

2

And marvelous rings in their tawny ears,
Which were pierced with the points of their shining spears.
To honor Heyóka, Wakáwa lifts
His fuming pipe from the Red-stone Quarry. ²³
The warriors follow. The white cloud drifts
From the Council-lodge to the welkin starry,
Like a fog at morn on the fir-clad hill,
When the meadows are damp and the winds are still.

They dance to the tune of their wild "Ha-ha!"
A warrior's shout and a raven's caw—
Circling the pot and the blazing fire
To the tom-tom's bray and the rude bassoon;
Round and round to their heart's desire,
And ever the same wild chant and tune—
A warrior's shout and a raven's caw—
"Ha-ha,—ha-ha,—ha-ha,—ha!"
They crouch, they leap, and their burning eyes
Flash fierce in the light of the flaming fire,
As fiercer and fiercer and higher and higher
The rude. wild notes of their chant arise.
They cease, they ,sit, and the curling smoke
Ascends again from their polished pipes,
And upward curls from their swarthy lips
To the god whose favor their hearts invoke.

Then tall Wakáwa arose and said:
"Brave warriors, listen, and give due heed.
Great is Heyóka, the magical god;
He can walk on the air; he can float on the flood.
He's a worker of magic and wonderful wise;
He cries when he laughs and he laughs when he cries;

He sweats when he's cold, and he shivers when hot,
And the water is cold in his boiling pot.
He hides in the earth and he walks in disguise,
But he loves the brave and their sacrifice.
We are sons of Heyòka. The Giant commands
In the boiling water to thrust our hands;
And the warrior that scorneth the foe and fire
Heyóka will crown with his heart's desire."

They thrust their hands in the boiling pot;
They swallow the bison-meat steaming hot;
Not a wince on their stoical faces bold,
For the meat and the water, they say, are cold;
And great is Heyóka and wonderful wise;
He floats on the flood and he walks in the skies,
And ever appears in a strange disguise;
But he loves the brave and their sacrifice;
And the warrior that scorneth the foe and fire
Heyóka will crown with his heart's desire.

Proud was the chief of his warriors proud,
The sinewy sons of the Giant's race:
But the bravest of all was the tall Red Cloud:
The eyes of the panther were set in his face;
He strode like a stag and he stood like a pine;
Ten feathers he wore of the great Wanmdeé; [13]
With crimsoned quills of the porcupine
His leggins were worked to his brawny knee.
Blood-red were the stripes on his swarthy cheek,
And the necklace that girdled his brawny neck
Was the polished claws of the great Mató [14]
He grappled and slew in the northern snow.

Proud Red Cloud turned to the braves and said,
As he shook the plumes on his 'haughty head:
"Ho! the warrior that scorneth the foe and fire
Heyóka will crown with his heart's desire!"
He snatched from the embers a red-hot brand,
And held it aloft in his naked hand.
He stood like a statue in bronze or stone,—
Not a muscle moved, and the braves looked on.
He turned to the chieftain,—"I scorn the fire,—
Ten feathers I wear of the great Wanmdeé;
Then grant me, Wakâwa, my heart's desire;
Let the sunlight shine in my lonely tee.[19]
I laugh at red death and I laugh at red fire;
Brave Red Cloud is only afraid of fear;
But Wiwâstè is fair to his heart and dear;
Then grant him, Wakâwa, his heart's desire."

The warriors applauded with loud "Ho! Ho!"[20]
And he flung the brand to the drifting snow.
Three times Wakâwa puffed forth the smoke
From his silent lips; then he slowly spoke:
"Mâhpíya is strong as the stout-armed oak
That stands on the bluff by the windy plain,
And laughs at the roar of the hurricane.
He has slain the foe and the great Mató
With his hissing arrow and deadly stroke.
My heart is swift but my tongue is slow.
Let the warrior come to my lodge and smoke;
He may bring the gifts;[21] but the timid doe
May fly from the hunter and say him no."

Wiwâstè sat late in the lodge alone,
Her dark eyes bent on the glowing fire.
She heard not the wild winds shrill and moan;
She heard not the tall elms toss and groan;
Her face was lit like the harvest moon;
For her thoughts flew far to her heart's desire.
Far away in the land of the Hóhé[15] dwelt
The warrior she held in her secret heart;
But little he dreamed of the pain she felt,
For she hid her love with a maiden's art.
Not a tear she shed, not a word she said,
When the fair young chief from the lodge departed;
But she sat on the mound when the day was dead,
And gazed at the full moon mellow - hearted.
Fair was the chief as the morning - star;
His eyes were mild and his words were low,
But his heart was stouter than lance or bow;
And her young heart flew to her love afar
O'er his trail long covered with drifted snow.
But she heard a warrior's stealthy tread,
And the tall Wakâwa appeared, and said—
"Is Wiwâstè afraid of the spirit dread
That fires the sky in the fatal north?[26]
Behold the mysterious lights. Come forth.
Some evil threatens,—some danger nears,
For the skies are pierced with the burning spears."

The warriors rally beneath the moon;
They shoot their shafts at the evil spirit.
The spirit is slain and the flame is gone,
And his blood lies red on the snow - fields near it.

But again from the dead will the spirit rise.
And flash his spears in the northern skies.

Then the chief and the queenly Wiwâstè stood
Alone in the moon-lit solitude,
And she was silent and he was grave.
"And fears not my daughter the evil spirit?
The strongest warriors and bravest fear it.
The burning spears are an evil omen;
They threaten the wrath of a wicked woman,
Or a treacherous foe; but my warriors brave,
When danger nears, or the foe appears,
Are a cloud of arrows.—a grove of spears."

"My Father," she said, and her words were low,
"Why should I fear? for I soon will go
To the broad, blue lodge in the Spirit-land,
Where my dark-eyed mother went long ago,
And my dear twin sisters walk hand in hand.
My Father, listen,—my words are true,"
And sad was her voice as the whippowil
When she mourns her mate by the moon-lit rill,
"Wiwâstè lingers alone with you;
The rest are sleeping on yonder hill,—
Save one—and he an undutiful son,—
And you, my Father, will sit alone
When Sisóka* sings and the snow is gone.
I sat, when the maple leaves were red,
By the foaming falls of the haunted river;
The night-sun was walking above my head,
And the arrows shone in his burnished quiver;

And the winds were hushed and the hour was dread
With the walking ghosts of the silent dead.
I heard the voice of the Water - Fairy;[29]
I saw her form in the moon-lit mist.
As she sat on a stone with her burden weary,
By the foaming eddies of amethyst.
And robed in her mantle of mist the sprite
Her low wail poured on the silent night.
Then the spirit spake, and the floods were still—
They hushed and listened to what she said,
And hushed was the plaint of the whippowil
In the silver-birches above her head:
'Wiwâstè.—the prairies are green and fair,
When the robin sings and the whippowil:
But the land of the Spirits is fairer still,
For the winds of winter blow never there;
And forever the songs of the whippowils
And the robins are heard on the leafy hills.
Thy mother looks from her lodge above,—
Her fair face shines in the sky afar,
And the eyes of thy sisters are bright with love,
As they peep from the tee of the mother-star.
To her happy lodge in the spirit-land
She beckons Wiwâstè with shining hand.'

"My Father,—my Father. her words were true;
And the death of Wiwâstè will rest on you.
You have pledged me as wife to the tall Red Cloud;
You will take the gifts of the warrior proud;
But I, Wakâwa,—I answer—never!
I will stain your knife in my heart's red blood,

I will plunge and sink in the sullen river,
Ere I will be wife to the fierce Red Cloud!"

"Wiwâstè," he said, and his voice was low,
"Let it be as you will, for Wakâwa's tongue
Has spoken no promise;—his lips are slow,
And the love of a father is deep and strong.
Be happy, Micúnksee[29]; the flames are gone,—
They flash no more in the Northern sky.
See the smile on the face of the watching moon;
No more will the fatal red arrows fly;
For the singing shafts of my warriors sped
To the bad spirit's bosom and laid him dead,
And his blood on the snow of the North lies red.
Go,—sleep in the robe that you won to-day,
And dream of your hunter—the brave Chaskè."

Light was her heart as she turned away;
It sang like the lark in the skies of May.
The round moon laughed, but a lone red star,[30]
As she turned to the teepee and entered in,
Fell flashing and swift in the sky afar,
Like the polished point of a javelin.
Nor chief nor daughter the shadow saw
Of the crouching listener—Hârpstinà.

Wiwâstè, wrapped in her robe and sleep
Heard not the storm-sprites wail and weep,
As they rode on the winds in the frosty air;
But she heard the voice of her hunter fair;
For a shadowy spirit with fairy fingers
The curtains drew from the land of dreams;

And lo in her teepee her lover lingers;
The light of love in his dark eye beams,
And his voice is the music of mountain streams.

And then with her round, brown arms she pressed
His phantom form to her throbbing breast,
And whispered the name, in her happy sleep,
Of her Hóhé hunter so fair and far.
And then she saw in her dreams the deep
Where the spirit wailed, and a falling star;
Then stealthily crouching under the trees,
By the light of the moon, the Kan-ó-ti-dan,[31]
The little, wizened, mysterious man,
With his long locks tossed by the moaning breeze,
Then a flap of wings, like a thunder-bird,[32]
And a wailing spirit the sleeper heard;
And lo, through the mists of the moon, she saw
The hateful visage of Hârpstinà.

But waking she murmured—"And what are these—
The flap of wings and the falling star,
The wailing spirit that's never at ease,
The little man crouching under the trees,
And the hateful visage of Hârpstinà?
My dreams are like feathers that float on the breeze,
And none can tell what the omens are—
Save the beautiful dream of my love afar
In the happy land of the tall Hóhé[15]—
My beautiful hunter—my brave Chaskè."

"Ta-tânka! Ta-tânka!"[33] the hunters cried,
With a joyous shout at the break of dawn;
And darkly lined on the white hill-side,

A herd of bison went marching on
Through the drifted snow like a caravan.
Swift to their ponies the hunters sped,
And dashed away on the hurried chase.
The wild steeds scented the game ahead,
And sprang like hounds to the eager race.
But the brawny bulls in the swarthy van
Turned their polished horns to the charging foes,
And reckless rider and fleet foot-man
Were held at bay in the drifted snows,
While the bellowing herd o'er the hill-tops ran,
Like the frightened beasts of a caravan
On the Sah'ra's sands when the simoon blows.
Sharp were the twangs of the hunters' bows,
And swift and humming the arrows sped, '
Till ten huge bulls on the bloody snows
Lay pierced with arrows and dumb and dead.
But the chief with the flankers had gained the rear,
And flew on the trail of the flying herd.
The shouts of the riders rang loud and clear,
As their frothing steeds to the chase they spurred.
And now like the roar of an avalanche
Rolls the sullen wrath of the maddened bulls.
They charge on the riders and runners stanch,
And a dying steed in the snow-drift rolls,
While the rider, flung to the frozen ground,
Escapes the horns by a panther's bound.
But the raging monsters are held at bay,
While the flankers dash on the swarthy rout.
With lance and arrow they slay and slay;

And the welkin rings to the gladsome shout—
To the loud Inâs and the wild Ihós, [31]—
And dark and dead, on the bloody snows,
Lie the swarthy heaps of the buffaloes.

All snug in the teepee Wiwâstè lay,
All wrapped in her robe, at the dawn of day,—
All snug and warm from the wind and snow,
While the hunters followed the buffalo.
Her dreams and her slumber their wild shouts broke;
The chase was afoot when the maid awoke:
She heard the twangs of the hunter's bows,
And the bellowing bulls and the loud Ihós,
And she murmured—"My hunter is far away
In the happy land of the tall Hóhé—
My beautiful hunter, my brave Chaskè;
But the robins will come and my warrior too,
And Wiwâstè will find her a way to woo."

And long she lay in a reverie,
And dreamed, wide-awake, of her brave Chaskè.
Till a trampling of feet on the crispy snow
She heard, and the murmur of voices low;—
Then the hunters' greeting—Ihó! Ihó!
And behold, in the blaze of the risen day,
With the hunters that followed the buffalo,—
Came her beautiful hunter—her brave Chaskè.
Far south has he followed the bison-trail
With his band of warriors so brave and true.
Right glad is Wakâwa his friend to hail,
And Wiwâstè will find her a way to woo.

Tall and straight as the larch-tree stood
The manly form of the brave young chief,
And fair as the larch in its vernal leaf,
When the red fawn bleats in the feathering wood.
Mild was his face as the morning skies,
And friendship shone in his laughing eyes;
But swift were his feet o'er the drifted snow
On the trail of the elk or the buffalo;
And his heart was stouter than lance or bow,
When he heard the whoop of his enemies.
Five feathers he wore of the great Wanmdeè,
And each for the scalp of a warrior slain,
When down on his camp from the northern plain,
With their murder-cries rode the bloody Cree. [45]
But never the stain of an infant slain,
Or the blood of a mother that plead in vain.
Soiled the honored plumes of the brave Hóhé.
A mountain bear to his enemies,
To his friends like the red fawn's dappled form;
In peace, like the breeze from the summer seas;
In war, like the roar of the mountain storm.
His fame in the voice of the winds went forth
From his hunting grounds in the happy north,
And far as the shores of the Great Medè [46]
The nations spoke of the brave Chaskè.

Dark was the visage of grim Red Cloud,
Fierce were the eyes of the warrior proud,
When the chief to his lodge led the brave Chaskè.
And Wiwâstè smiled on the tall Hóhé.

Away he strode with a sullen frown,
And alone in his teepee he sat him down.
From the gladsome greeting of braves he stole,
And wrapped himself in his gloomy soul.
But the eagle eyes of the Hárpstinà
The clouded face of the warrior saw.
Softly she spoke to the sullen brave:
"Mah-pí-ya Dúta,—his face is sad.
And why is the warrior so glum and grave?
For the fair Wiwâstè is gay and glad.
She will sit in the teepee the live-long day,
And laugh with her lover—the brave Hóhé.
Does the tall Red Cloud for the false one sigh?
There are fairer maidens than she, and proud
Were their hearts to be loved by the brave Red Cloud.
And trust not the chief with the smiling eyes;
His tongue is swift, but his words are lies;
And the proud Mah pí-ya will surely find
That Wahâwa's promise is hollow wind.
Last night I stood by his lodge, and lo
I heard the voice of the Little Crow;
But the fox is sly and his words were low.
But I heard her answer her father—"Never!
I will stain your knife in my heart's red blood,
I will plunge and sink in the sullen river,
Ere I will be wife to the fierce Red Cloud!"
Then he spake again, and his voice was low,
But I heard the answer of Little Crow:
"Let it be as you will, for Wakâwa's tongue
Has spoken no promise,—his lips are slow,
And the love of a father is deep and strong."

Mah-pí-ya Dúta, they scorn your love,
But the false chief covets the warrior's gifts.
False to his promise the fox will prove,
And fickle as snow in Wo-ká-da-weè, [37]
That slips into brooks when the gray cloud lifts,
Or the red sun looks through the ragged rifts.
Mah-pí-ya Dúta will listen to me.
There are fairer birds in the bush than she,
And the fairest would gladly be Red Cloud's wife.
Will the warrior sit like a girl bereft,
When fairer and truer than she are left
That love Red Cloud as they love their life?
Mah-pí-ya Dúta will listen to me.
I love him well,—I have loved him long:
A woman is weak, but a warrior is strong,
And a love-lorn brave is a scorn to see.

Mah-pí-ya Dúta, O listen to me!
Revenge is swift and revenge is strong,
And sweet as the hive in the hollow tree.
The proud Red Cloud will revenge his wrong:
Let the brave be patient, it is not long
Till the leaves be green on the maple tree,
And the Feast of the Virgins is then to be;—
The Feast of the Virgins is then to be!"

Proudly she turned from the silent brave,
And went her way; but the warrior's eyes—
They flashed with the flame of a sudden fire,
Like the lights that gleam in the Sacred Cave, [38]
When the black night covers the autumn skies,
And the stars from their welkin watch retire.

Three nights he tarried—the brave Chaskè;
Winged were the hours and they flitted away;
On the wings of Wakândee[39] they silently flew,
For Wiwâstè had found her a way to woo.
Ah little he cared for the bison-chase;
For the red lilies bloomed on the fair maid's face;
Ah little he cared for the winds that blew,
For Wiwâstè had found her a way to woo.
Brown-bosomed she sat on her fox-robe dark,
Her ear to the tales of the brave inclined,
Or tripped from the tee like the song of a lark,
And gathered her hair from the wanton wind.
Ah, little he thought of the leagues of snow
He trode on the trail of the buffalo;
And little he recked of the hurricanes
That swept the snow from the frozen plains
And piled the banks of the Bloody River.[40]
His bow unstrung and forgotten hung
With his beaver hood and his otter quiver:
He sat spell-bound by the artless grace
Of her star-lit eyes and her moon-lit face.
Ah little he cared for the storms that blew,
For Wiwâstè had found her a way to woo.
When he spoke with Wakâwa her sidelong eye
Sought the handsome chief in his hunter-guise.
Wakâwa marked, and the lilies fair
On her round cheeks spread to her raven hair.
They feasted on rib of the bison fat,
On the tongue of the Ta[41] that the hunters prize,
On the savory flesh of the red Hogân,[42]
On sweet tipsânna[43] and pemmican,

And the dun-brown cakes of the golden maize;
And hour after hour the young chief sat,
And feasted his soul on the maiden's eyes.

The sweeter the moments the swifter they fly;
Love takes no account of the fleeting hours;
He walks in a dream mid the blooming of flowers,
And never awakes till the blossoms die.
Ah, lovers are lovers the wide world over—
In the hunter's lodge and the royal palace.
Sweet are the lips of his love to the lover,—
Sweet as new wine in a golden chalice,
From the Tajo's⁴⁴ slopes or the hills beyond;
And blindly he sips from his loved one's lips,
In lodge or palace the wide world over,
The maddening honey of Trebizond.⁴⁵

O what are leagues to the loving hunter,
Or the blinding drift of the hurricane,
When it raves and roars o'er the frozen plain!
He would face the storm,—he would death encounter
The darling prize of his heart to gain,
But his hunters chafed at the long delay,
For the swarthy bison were far away,
And the brave young chief from the lodge departed.
He promised to come with the robin in May,
With the bridal gifts for the bridal day;
And the fair Wiwâstè was happy-hearted,
For Wakâwa promised the brave Chaskè.

Birds of a feather will flock together,
The robin sings to his ruddy mate,

And the chattering jays, in the winter weather,
To prate and gossip will congregate;
And the cawing crows on the autumn heather,
Like evil omens, will flock together,
In extra-session, for high debate;
And the lass will slip from a doting mother
To hang with her lad on the garden gate.
Birds of a feather will flock together.—
'Tis an adage old,—it is nature's law,
And sure as the pole will the needle draw.
The fierce Red Cloud with the flaunting feather,
Will follow the finger of Hârpstinà.

The winter wanes and the south-wind blows
From the Summer Islands legendary.
The skéskas[16] fly and the melted snows
In lakelets lie on the dimpled prairie.
The frost-flowers[17] peep from their winter sleep
Under the snow-drifts cold and deep.

To the April sun and the April showers,
In field and forest, the baby flowers
Lift their golden faces and azure eyes;
And wet with the tears of the winter-fairies,
Soon bloom and blossom the emerald prairies,
Like the fabled Garden of Paradise.

The plum-trees, white with their bloom in May,
Their sweet perfume on the vernal breeze
Wide strew like the isles of the tropic seas,
Where the paroquet chatters the livelong day.
But the May-days pass and the brave Chaskè—

3

O why does the lover so long delay?
Wiwâstè waits in the lonely tee.
Has her fair face fled from his memory?
For the robin cherups his mate to please,
The blue-bird pipes in the poplar-trees.   .
The meadow-lark warbles his jubilees,
Shrilling his song in the azure seas.
Till the welkin throbs to his melodies;
And low is the hum of the humble-bees.
And the Feast of the Virgins is now to be.

THE FEAST OF THE VIRGINS.

The sun sails high in his azure realms;
Beneath the arch of the breezy elms
The feast is spread by the murmuring river.
With his battle-spear and his bow and quiver,
And eagle-plumes in his ebon hair,
The chief Wakâwa himself is there;
And round the feast, in · the Sacred Ring, [48]
Sit his weaponed warriors witnessing.
Not a morsel of food have the Virgins tasted
For three long days ere the holy feast;
They sat in their teepee alone and fasted,
Their faces turned to the Sacred East. [21]
In the polished bowls lies the golden maize.
And the flesh of fawn on the polished trays.
For the Virgins the bloom of the prairies wide—
The blushing pink and the meek blue-bell,

The purple plumes of the prairie's pride,⁴⁹
The wild, uncultured asphodel,
And the beautiful. blue-eyed violet
That the Virgins call "Let-me-not-forget,"
In gay festoons and garlands twine
With the cedar sprigs⁵⁰ and the wildwood vine.
So gaily the Virgins are decked and dressed,
And none but a virgin may enter there:
And clad is each in a scarlet vest,
And a fawn-skin frock to the brown calves bare:
Wild rose-buds peep from their flowing hair.
And a rose half-blown on the budding breast;
And bright with the quills of the porcupine
The moccasined feet of the maidens shine.

Hand in hand round the feast they dance.
And sing to the notes of a rude bassoon,
And never a pause or a dissonance
In the merry dance or the merry tune.
Brown-bosomed and fair as the rising moon.
When she peeps o'er the hills of the dewy east,
Wiwâstè sings at the Virgins' Feast;
And bright is the light in her luminous eyes;
They glow like the stars in the winter skies:
And the lilies that bloom in her virgin heart
Their golden blush to her cheeks impart—
Her cheeks half-hid in her midnight hair.
Fair is her form—as the red fawn's fair.
And long is the flow of her raven hair;
It falls to her knees, and it streams on the breeze
Like the path of a storm on the swelling seas.

Proud of their rites are the Virgins fair.
For none but a virgin may enter there.
'Tis a custom of old and a sacred thing:
Nor rank nor beauty the warriors spare.
If a tarnished maiden should enter there.
And her that enters the Sacred Ring
With a blot that is known or a secret stain
The warrior who knows is bound to expose,
And lead her forth from the ring again.
And the word of the warrior is sacred by law;
For the Virgins' Feast is a sacred thing.
Aside with the mothers sat Hârpstinà;
She durst not enter the Virgins' ring.

Round and round to the merry song
The maidens dance in their gay attire.
While the loud "Ho-Ho's" of the tawny throng
Their flying feet and their song inspire.
They have finished the song and the sacred dance,
And hand in hand to the feast advance—
To the polished bowls of the golden maize,
And the sweet fawn-meat in the polished trays.

Then up from his seat in the silent crowd
Rose the frowning, fierce-eyed, tall Red Cloud;
Swift was his stride as the panther's spring,
When he leaps on the fawn from his cavern lair;
Wiwâstè he caught by her flowing hair,
And dragged her forth from the Sacred Ring.
She turned on the warrior. Her eyes flashed fire;
Her proud lips quivered with queenly ire;

Her hand to the spirits she raised and said,
And her sun-browned cheeks were aflame with red:
"I am pure!—I am pure as the falling snow!
Great Tâku-skan-skan [31] will testify!
And dares the tall coward to say me no?"
But the sullen warrior made no reply.
She turned to the chief with her frantic cries:
"Wakâwa,—my Father; he lies,—he lies!
Wiwâstè is pure as the fawn unborn;
Lead me back to the feast, or Wiwâstè dies!"
But the warriors uttered a cry of scorn,
And he turned his face from her pleading eyes.

Then the sullen warrior, the tall Red Cloud,
Looked up and spoke and his voice was loud;
But he held his wrath and he spoke with care:
"Wiwâstè is young; she is proud and fair,
But she may not boast of the virgin snows.
The Virgins' Feast is a sacred thing;
How durst she enter the Virgins' ring?
The warrior would fain, but he dares not spare;
She is tarnished and only the Red Cloud knows."

She clutched her hair in her clenchèd hand;
She stood like a statue bronzed and grand:
Wakân-deè [30] flashed in her fiery eyes:
Then swift as the meteor cleaves the skies,—
Nay, swift as the fiery Wakínyan's dart, [32]
She snatched the knife from the warrior's belt,
And plunged it clean to the polished hilt—
With a deadly cry—in the villain's heart.
Staggering he clutched the air and fell;

His life-blood smoked on the trampled sand,
And dripped from the knife in the virgin's hand.
Then rose his kinsmen's savage yell.
Swift as the doe's Wiwâstè's feet
Fled away to the forest.   The hunters fleet
In vain pursue, and in vain they prowl.
And lurk in the forest till dawn of day.
They hear the hoot of the mottled owl:
They hear the were-wolf's⁵² winding howl;
But the swift Wiwâstè is far away.
They found no trace in the forest land,
They found no trail in the dew-damp grass,
They found no track in the river sand,
Where they thought Wiwâstè would surely pass.

The braves returned to the troubled chief;
In his lodge he sat in his silent grief.
"Surely," they said, "she has turned a spirit.
No trail she left with her flying feet;
No pathway leads to her far retreat.
She flew in the air, and her wail—we could hear it,
As she upward rose to the shining stars;
And we heard on the river, as we stood near it,
The falling drops of Wiwâstè's tears."

Wakâwa thought of his daughter's words
Ere the south-wind came and the piping birds—
"My Father, listen,—my words are true,"
And sad was her voice as the whippowil
When she mourns her mate by the moon-lit rill,
"Wiwâstè lingers alone with you:

The rest are sleeping on yonder hill—
Save one—and he an undutiful son,—
And you, my Father, will sit alone
When Sisóka[59] sings and the snow is gone."
His broad breast heaved on his troubled soul,
The shadow of grief o'er his visage stole
Like a cloud on the face of the setting sun.

"She has followed the years that are gone," he said;
"The spirits the words of the witch fulfill;
For I saw the ghost of my father dead,
By the moon's dim light on the misty hill.
He shook the plumes on his withered head,
And the wind through his pale form whistled shrill.
And a low, sad voice on the hill I heard,
Like the mournful wail of a widowed bird."
Then lo, as he looked from his lodge afar,
He saw the glow of the Evening-star;
".And yonder," he said, "is Wiwâstè's face;
She looks from her lodge on our fading race.
Devoured by famine, and fraud, and war,
And chased and hounded from woe to woe,
As the white wolves follow the buffalo."
And he named the planet the *Virgin Star.*[54]

"Wakâwa," he muttered, "the guilt is thine!
She was pure,—she was pure as the fawn unborn.
O why did I hark to the cry of scorn,
Or the words of the lying libertine?
Wakâwa, Wakâwa, the guilt is thine!
The springs will return with the voice of birds,
But the voice of my daughter will come no more.

She wakened the woods with her musical words,
And the sky-lark, ashamed of his voice, forbore.
She called back the years that had passed, and long
I heard their voice in her happy song.
Her heart was the home of the sunbeam. Bright
Poured the stream of her song on the starry night.
O why did the chief of the tall Hóhé
His feet from Kapóza° so long delay?
For his father sat at my father's feast,
And he at Wakâwa's—an honored guest.
He is dead!—he is slain on the Bloody Plain,
By the hand of the treacherous Chippeway;
And the face shall I never behold again
Of my brave young brother—the chief Chaskè.
Death walks like a shadow among my kin;
And swift are the feet of the flying years
That cover Wakâwa with frost and tears,
And leave their tracks on his wrinkled skin.
Wakâwa. the voice of the years that are gone
Will follow thy feet like the shadow of death,
Till the paths of the forest and desert lone
Shall forget thy footsteps. O living breath,
Whence art thou, and whither so soon to fly?
And whence are the years? Shall I overtake
Their flying feet in the star-lit sky?
From his last long sleep will the warrior wake?
Will the morning break in Wakâwa's tomb,
As it breaks and glows in the eastern skies?
Is it true?—will the spirits of kinsmen come
And bid the bones of the brave arise?

"Wakâwa. Wakâwa, for thee the years
Are red with blood and bitter with tears.
Gone,—brothers, and daughters, and wife,—all gone
That are kin to Wakâwa,—but one—but one—
Wakínyan Tânka—undutiful son !
And he estranged from his father's tee,
Will never return till the chief shall die.
And what cares he for his father's grief ?
He will smile at my death.—it will make him chief.
Woe burns in my bosom. Ho. Warriors,—Ho !
Raise the song of red war; for your chief must go
To drown his grief in the blood of the foe !
I shall fall. Raise my mound on the sacred hill.
Let my warriors the wish of their chief fulfill ;
For my fathers sleep in the sacred ground. .
The Autumn blasts o'er Wakâwa's mound
Shall chase the hair of the thistle's head,
And the bare-armed oak o'er the silent dead,
When the whirling snows from the north descend,
Shall wail and moan in the midnight wind.
In the famine of winter the wolf shall prowl.
And scratch the snow from the heap of stones.
And sit in the gathering storm and howl,
On the frozen mound, for Wakâwa's bones.
But the years that are gone shall return again,
As the robin returns and the whippowil.
When my warriors stand on the sacred hill
And remember the deeds of their brave chief slain. "

Beneath the glow of the Virgin Star
They raised the song of the red war-dance.

At the break of dawn with the bow and lance
They followed the chief on the path of war.
To the north—to the forests of fir and pine—
Led their stealthy steps on the winding trail,
Till they saw the Lake of the Spirit [55] shine
Through somber pines of the dusky dale.
Then they heard the hoot of the mottled owl; [56]
They heard the gray wolf's dismal howl;
Then shrill and sudden the war-whoop rose
From an hundred throats of their swarthy foes.
In ambush crouched in the tangled wood.
Death shrieked in the twang of their deadly bows,
And their hissing arrows drank brave men's blood.
From rock, and thicket, and brush, and brakes,
Gleamed the burning eyes of the forest-snakes. [57]
From brake, and thicket, and brush, and stone,
The bow-string hummed and the arrow hissed,
And the lance of a crouching Ojibway shone,
Or the scalp-knife gleamed in a swarthy fist.
Undaunted the braves of Wakâwa's band
Leaped into the thicket with lance and knife,
And grappled the Chippewas hand to hand;
And foe with foe, in the deadly strife,
Lay clutching the scalp of his foe and dead.
With a tomahawk sunk in his ghastly head,
Or his still heart sheathing a bloody blade.
Like a bear in the battle Wakâwa raves.
And cheers the hearts of his falling braves.
But a panther crouches along his track,—
He springs with a yell on Wakâwa's back!

The tall Chief, stabbed to the heart, lies low;
But his left hand clutches his deadly foe.
And his red right clenches the bloody hilt
Of his knife in the heart of the slayer dyed.
And thus was the life of Wakâwa spilt,
And slain and slayer lay side by side.
The unscalped corpse of their honored chief
His warriors snatched from the yelling pack,
And homeward fled on their forest track
With their bloody burden and load of grief.

The spirits the words of the brave fulfill,—
Wakâwa sleeps on the sacred hill,
And Wakínyan Tânka, his son, is chief.
Ah, soon shall the lips of men forget
Wakâwa's name, and the mound of stone
Will speak of the dead to the winds alone,
And the winds will whistle their mock-regret.

The speckled cones of the scarlet berries[58]
Lie red and ripe in the prairie grass.
The Sí-yo[59] clucks on the emerald prairies
To her infant brood. From the wild morass,
On the sapphire lakelet set within it,
Magâ[60] sails forth with her wee ones daily.
They ride on the dimpling waters gaily,
Like a fleet of yachts and a man-of-war.
The piping plover, the laughing linnet,
And the swallow sail in the sunset skies.
The whippowil from her cover hies,
And trills her song on the amber air.

Anon to her loitering mate she cries
"Flip. O Will!—trip, O Will!—skip, O Will!"
And her merry mate from afar replies:
"Flip I will,—skip I will,—trip I will;"
And away on the wings of the wind he flies.
And bright from her lodge in the skies afar
Peeps the glowing face of the Virgin Star.
The fox-pups[60] creep from the mother's lair,
And leap in the light of the rising moon;
And loud on the luminous, moonlit lake
Shrill the bugle-notes of the lover loon;
And woods and waters and welkin break
Into jubilant song,—it is joyful June.

But where is Wiwâstè? O where is she—
The Virgin avenged—the queenly queen—
The womanly woman—the heroine?
Has she gone to the spirits, and can it be
That her beautiful face is the Virgin Star
Peeping out from the door of her lodge afar,
Or upward sailing the silver sea,
Star-beaconed and lit like an avenue,
In the shining stern of her gold canoe?
No tidings came.—nor the brave Chaskè:
O why did the lover so long delay?
He promised to come with the robins in May,
With the bridal gifts for the bridal day;
But the fair May-mornings have slipped away.
And where is the lover—the brave Chaskè?

But what of the venomous Hârpstinà—
The serpent that tempted the proud Red Cloud,

And kindled revenge in his savage soul?
He paid for his crime with his false heart's blood,
But his angry spirit has brought her dole;[61]
It has entered her breast and her burning head,
And she raves and burns on her fevered bed.
"He is dead! He is dead!" is her wailing cry.
"And the blame is mine,—it was I,—it was I!
I hated Wiwâstè, for she was fair,
And my brave was caught in her net of hair.
I turned his love to a bitter hate;
I nourished revenge. and I pricked his pride;
Till the Feast of the Virgins I bade him wait.
He had his revenge, but he died,—he died!
And the blame is mine,—it was I,—it was I!
And his spirit burns me; I die,—I die!"
Thus, alone in her lodge and her agonies,
She wails to the winds of the night, and dies.

But where is Wiwâstè? Her swift feet flew
To the somber shades of the tangled thicket.
She hid in the copse like a wary cricket,
And the fleetest hunters in vain pursue.
Seeing unseen from her hiding place,
She sees them fly on the hurried chase;
She sees their fierce eyes glance and dart.
As they pass and peer for a track or trace,
And she trembles with fear in the copse apart,
Lest her nest be betrayed by her throbbing heart.

Weary the hours; but the sun at last
Went down to his lodge in the west, and fast

The wings of the spirits of night were spread
O'er the darkling woods and Wiwáste's head.
Then slyly she slipped from her snug retreat,
And guiding her course by Waziya's star,"²
That shone through the shadowy forms afar.
She northward hurried with silent feet;
And long ere the sky was aflame in the east,
She was leagues from the place of the fatal feast.
'Twas the hoot of the owl that the hunters heard.
And the scattering drops of the threat'ning shower.
And the far wolf's cry to the moon preferred.
Their ears were their fancies,—the scene was weird,
And the witches'³ dance at the midnight hour.
She leaped the brook and she swam the river;
Her course through the forest Wiwáste wist

By the star that gleamed through the glimmering mist
That fell from the dim moon's downy quiver.
In her heart she spoke to her spirit-mother:
"Look down from your teepee, O starry spirit,
The cry of Wiwâstè, O mother, hear it;
And touch the heart of my cruel father.
He hearkened not to a virgin's words;
He listened not to a daughter's wail.
O give me the wings of the thunder-birds,
For his were-wolves[52] follow Wiwâstè's trail;
O guide my flight to the far Hóhé—
To the sheltering lodge of my brave Chaskè."

The shadows paled in the hazy east,
And the light of the kindling morn increased.
The pale-faced stars fled one by one,
And hid in the vast from the rising sun.
From woods and waters and welkin soon
Fled the hovering mists of the vanished moon.
The young robins chirped in their feathery beds,
The loon's song shrilled like a winding horn,
And the green hills lifted their dewy heads
To greet the god of the rising morn.

She reached the rim of the rolling prairie—
The boundless ocean of solitude;
She hid in the feathery hazel-wood,
For her heart was sick and her feet were weary;
She fain would rest, and she needed food.
Alone by the billowy, boundless prairies,
She plucked the cones of the scarlet berries;
In feathering copse and the grassy field

She found the bulbs of the young Tipsânna,⁵⁹
And the sweet medó⁶⁰ that the meadows yield.
With the precious gift of his priceless manna
God fed his fainting and famished child.

At night again to the northward far
She followed the torch of Waźíya's star.
For leagues away o'er the prairies green,
On the billowy vast, may a man be seen,
When the sun is high and the stars are low;
And the sable breast of the strutting crow
Looms up like the form of the buffalo.
The Bloody River⁶¹ she reached at last,
And boldly walked in the light of day,
On the level plain of the valley vast;
Nor thought of the terrible Chippeway.
She was safe from the wolves of her father's band,
But she trode on the treacherous "Bloody Land."

And lo—from afar o'er the level plain—
As far as the sails of a ship at sea
May be seen as they lift from the rolling main—
A band of warriors rode rapidly.
She shadowed her eyes with her sun-browned hand;
All backward streamed on the wind her hair,
And terror spread o'er her visage fair,
As she bent her brow to the far-off band.
For she thought of the terrible Chippeway—
The fiends that the babe and the mother slay;
And yonder they came in their war-array!
She hid like a grouse in the meadow-grass,
And moaned—"I am lost!—I am lost! alas:

And why did I fly from my native land
To die by the cruel Ojibway's hand?"
And on rode the braves. She could hear the steeds
Come galloping on o'er the level meads;
And lowly she crouched in the waving grass,
And hoped against hope that the braves would pass.

They have passed; she is safe,—she is safe! Ah, no;
They have struck her trail and the hunters halt.
Like wolves on the track of the bleeding doe,
That grappled breaks from the dread assault,
Dash the warriors wild on Wiwâstè's trail.
She flies,—but what can her flight avail?
Her feet are fleet, but the flying feet
Of the steeds of the prairies are fleeter still;
And where can she fly for a safe retreat?

But hark to the shouting:—"Ihó!—Ihó!"³
Rings over the wide plain sharp and shrill.
She halts, and the hunters come riding on;
But the horrible fear from her heart is gone,
For it is not the shout of the dreaded foe;
'Tis the welcome shout of her native land!

Up galloped the chief of the band, and lo—
The clutched knife dropped from her trembling hand;
She uttered a cry and she swooned away;
For there, on his steed in the blaze of day,
On the boundless prairie, so far away,
With his burnished lance and his feathers gay,
Sat the manly form of her own Chaskè!

4

There's a mote in my eye or a blot on the page,
And I cannot tell of the joyful greeting;
You may take it for granted and I will engage,
There were kisses and tears at the strange, glad meeting;
For aye since the birth of the swift-winged years.
In the desert drear, in the field of clover,
In the cot, and the palace, and all the world over,—
Yea, away on the stars to the ultimate spheres,
The language of love to the long-sought lover,—
Is tears and kisses and kisses and tears.

But why did the lover so long delay?
And whitherward rideth the chief to-day?
As he followed the trail of the buffalo.
From the tees of Kapóza a maiden, lo,
Came running in haste o'er the drifted snow.
She spoke to the chief of the tall Hóhè:
"Wiwâstè requests that the brave Chaskè
Will abide with his band and his coming delay
'Till the moon when the strawberries are ripe and red,
And then will the chief and Wiwâstè wed—
When the Feast of the Virgins is past," she said.
Wiwâstè's wish was her lover's law;
And so his coming the chief delayed
Till the mid-May blossoms should bloom and fade,—
But the lying runner was Hârpstinà.

And now with the gifts for the bridal day
And his chosen warriors he took his way,
And followed his heart to his moon-faced maid.
And thus was the lover so long delayed;

And so as he rode with his warriors gay,
On that bright and beautiful summer day,
His bride he met on the trail mid-way,
By the haunts of the treacherous Chippeway.

God arms the innocent. He is there—
In the desert vast, in the wilderness,
On the bellowing sea, in the lion's lair,
In the midst of battle, and everywhere.
In his hand he holds with a father's care
The tender hearts of the motherless;
The maid and the mother in sore distress
He shields with his love and his tenderness;
He comforts the widowed—the comfortless,
And sweetens her chalice of bitterness;
He clothes the naked—the numberless,—
His charity covers their nakedness.—
And he feeds the famished and fatherless
With the hand that feedeth the birds of air.
Let the myriad tongues of the earth confess
His infinite love and his holiness;
For his pity pities the pitiless,
His wayward children his bounties bless,
And his mercy flows to the merciless:
And the countless worlds in the realms above,
Revolve in the light of his boundless love.

And what of the lovers? you ask, I trow.
She told him all ere the sun was low,—
Why she fled from the Feast to a safe retreat.
She laid her heart at her lover's feet,

And her words were tears and her lips were slow.
As she sadly related the bitter tale
His face was aflame and anon grew pale,
And his dark eyes flashed with a brave desire,
Like the midnight gleam of the sacred fire.[65]
"Mitâwin,"[66] he said, and his voice was low,
"Thy father no more is the false Little Crow;
But the fairest plume shall Wiwâstè wear
Of the great Wanmdeè[13] in her midnight hair.
In my lodge, in the land of the tall Hóhè,
The robins will sing all the long summer day
To the beautiful bride of the brave Chaskè."

Aye, love is tested by stress and trial
Since the finger of time on the endless dial
Began its rounds, and the orbs to move
In the boundless vast, and the sunbeams clove
The chaos; but only by fate's denial
Is fathomed the fathomless depths of love.
Man is the rugged and wrinkled oak,
And woman the trusting and tender vine—
That clasps and climbs till its arms entwine
The brawny arms of the sturdy stoke.[67]
The dimpled babes are the flowers divine
That the blessing of God on the vine and oak
With their cooing and blossoming lips invoke.

To the pleasant land of the brave Hóhè
Wiwâstè rode with her proud Chaskè.
She ruled like a queen in his bountiful tee,
And the life of the twain was a jubilee.

Their wee ones climbed on the father's knee,
And played with his plumes of the great Wanmdeè.
The silken threads of the happy years
They wove into beautiful robes of love
That the spirits wear in the lodge above;
And time from the reel of the rolling spheres
His silver threads with the raven wove;
But never the stain of a mother's tears
Soiled the shining web of their happy years.

When the wrinkled mask of the years they wore,
And the raven hair of their youth was gray,
Their love grew deeper, and more and more;
For he was a lover for aye and aye,
And ever her beautiful, brave Chaskè.
Through the wrinkled mask of the hoary years
To the loving eyes of the lover aye
The blossom of beautiful youth appears.

At last, when their locks were as white as snow,
Beloved and honored by all the band,
They silently slipped from their lodge below,
And walked together, and hand in hand,
O'er the Shining Path[63] to the Spirit-land;
Where the hills and the meadows for aye and aye
Are clad with the verdure and flowers of May,
And the unsown prairies of Paradise
Yield the golden maize and the sweet wild-rice.
There ever ripe in the groves and prairies
Hang the purple plums and the luscious berries.

And the swarthy herds of the bison feed
On the sun-lit slope and the waving mead;
The dappled fawns from their coverts peep,
And countless flocks on the waters sleep;
And the silent years with their fingers trace
No furrows for aye on the hunter's face.

WINONA.

FALLS OF ST. ANTHONY.

Fac Simile of the Cut in Carver's Travels, published at London, in 1778, from a Survey and Sketch made by Capt. J. Carver, Nov. 17, 1766. Perpendicular Fall, 30 Feet; Breadth near 600 Feet.

WINONA.[1]

When the meadow-lark trilled o'er the leas and the oriole piped in the maples,
From my hammock, all under the trees, by the sweet-scented field of red-clover,
I harked to the hum of the bees, as they gathered the mead of the blossoms,
And caught from their low melodies the rhythm of the song of Winona.

In pronouncing Dakota words give "a" the sound of "ah,"—"e" the sound of "a,"—"i" the sound of "e" and "u" the sound of "oo." Sound "ee" the same as in English. The numerals 1—2, etc., refer to notes in the appendix.)

Two hundred white Winters and more have fled from the face of the Summer,
Since here on the oak-shaded shore of the dark-winding, swift Mississippi,
Where his foaming floods tumble and roar, on the falls and the white-rolling rapids,
In the fair, fabled center of Earth, sat the Indian town of Ka-thá-ga.[80]
Far rolling away to the north, and the south, lay the emerald prairies,
Alternate with woodlands and lakes, and above them the blue vast of ether.
And here where the dark river breaks into spray and the roar of the Ha-Ha,[76]
Were gathered the bison-skin tees of the chief tawny tribe of Dakotas;
For here, in the blast and the breeze, flew the flag of the chief of Isantees,[80]
Up-raised on the stem of a lance—the feathery flag of the eagle.
And here to the feast and the dance, from the prairies remote and the forests,
Oft gathered the out-lying bands, and honored the gods of the nation.
On the islands and murmuring strands they danced to the god of the waters,
Unktéhee,[60] who dwelt in the caves, deep under the flood of the Ha-Ha;[76]
And high o'er the eddies and waves hung their offerings of furs and tobacco.*
And here to the Master of life—Anpé-tu-wee,[70] god of the heavens,
Chief, warrior, and maiden, and wife, burned the sacred green sprigs of the cedar.[50]
And here to the Searcher-of-hearts—fierce Tá-ku Skan-skán,[51] the avenger,
Who dwells in the uttermost parts—in the earth and the blue, starry ether,

*See Hennepin's Discription of Louisiana, by Shea, pp. 243 and 256. Parkman's Discovery, p. 246— and Carver's Travels, p. 67.

Ever watching, with all-seeing eyes, the deeds of the wives and the warriors,
As an osprey afar in the skies, sees the fish as they swim in the waters,
Oft spread they the bison-tongue feast, and singing preferred their petitions,
Till the Day-Spirit[70] rose in the East—in the red, rosy robes of the morning,
To sail o'er the sea of the skies, to his lodge in the land of the shadows,
Where the black-winged tornadoes* arise—rushing loud from the mouths of their caverns.
And here with a shudder they heard, flying far from his tee in the mountains,
Wa-kní-yan,[32] the huge Thunder-Bird, with the arrows of fire in his talons.

Two hundred white Winters and more have fled from the face of the Summer,
Since here by the cataract's roar, in the moon of the red-blooming lilies,[71]
In the tee of Ta-té-psin† was born Winona—wild-rose of the prairies.
Like the summer sun peeping, at morn, o'er the hills was the face of Winona;
And here she grew up like a queen—a romping and lily-lipped laughter,
And danced on the undulant green, and played in the frolicsome waters,
Where the foaming tide tumbles and twirls o'er the murmuring rocks in the rapids;
And whiter than foam were the pearls that gleamed in the midst of her laughter.
Long and dark was her flowing hair flung, like the robe of the night to the breezes;
And gay as the robin she sung, or the gold-breasted lark of the meadows.
Like the wings of the wind were her feet, and as sure as the feet of Ta-tó-ka;‡
And oft like an antelope fleet o'er the hills and the prairies she bounded,
Lightly laughing in sport as she ran, and looking back over her shoulder,
At the fleet-footed maiden or man, that vainly her flying steps followed.
The belle of the village was she, and the pride of the aged Ta-té-psin;
Like a sunbeam she lighted his tee, and gladdened the heart of her father.

In the golden-hued Wázu-pe-weé—the moon when the wild-rice is gathered;
When the leaves on the tall sugar-tree are as red as the breast of the robin,
And the red-oaks that border the lea are aflame with the fire of the sunset,
From the wide-waving fields of wild-rice—from the meadows of Psin-ta-wak-pá-dan,§

*The Dakotas, like the ancient Romans and Greeks, think the home of the winds is in the caverns of the mountains, and their great Thunder-bird resembles in many respects the Jupiter of the Romans and the Zeus of the Greeks. The resemblance of the Dakota mythology to that of the older Greeks and Romans is striking.

†Tate—wind,—psin—wild-rice—wild-rice wind.

‡The Mountain antelope.

§Little Rice River. It bears the name of Rice Creek to-day and empties into the Mississippi from the east, a few miles above Minneapolis.

Where the geese and the mallards rejoice, and grow fat on the bountiful harvest,
Came the hunters with saddles of moose and the flesh of the bear and the bison,
And the women in birchen canoes well laden with rice from the meadows,

With the tall, dusky hunters, behold, came a marvelous man or a spirit,
White-faced and so wrinkled and old, and clad in the robe of the raven.
Unsteady his steps were and slow, and he walked with a staff in his right hand,
And white as the first-falling snow were the thin locks that lay on his shoulders.
Like rime-covered moss hung his beard, flowing down from his face to his girdle;
And wan was his aspect and weird; and often he chanted and mumbled
In a strange and mysterious tongue, as he bent o'er his book in devotion,
Or lifted his dim eyes and sung, in a low voice, the solemn "*Te Deum.*"
Or Latin, or Hebrew, or Greek—all the same were his words to the warriors,—
All the same to the maids and the meek, wide-wondering-eyed, hazel-brown children.

Father René Menard*—it was he, long lost to his Jesuit brothers,
Sent forth by an holy decree to carry the Cross to the heathen.
In his old age abandoned to die, in the swamps, by his timid companions,
He prayed to the Virgin on high, and she led him forth from the forest;
For angels she sent him as men—in the forms of the tawny Dakotas,
And they led his feet from the fen,—from the slough of despond and the desert.
Half-dead in a dismal morass, as they followed the red-deer they found him,
In the midst of the mire and the grass, and mumbling "*Te Deum laudamus.*"
"Unktómee¹—Ho!" muttered the braves, for they deemed him the black Spider-Spirit
That dwells in the drearisome caves, and walks on the marshes at midnight,
With a flickering torch in his hand, to decoy to his den the unwary.
His tongue could they not understand, but his torn hands all shriveled with famine,
He stretched to the hunters and said: "He feedeth his chosen with manna;
And ye are the angels of God, sent to save me from death in the desert."
His famished and woe-begone face, and his tones touched the hearts of the hunters;
They fed the poor father apace, and they led him away to Ka-thá-ga.

There little by little he learned the tongue of the tawny Dakotas;
And the heart of the good father yearned to lead them away from their idols—
Their giants¹⁶ and dread Thunder-birds—their worship of stones⁷³ and the devil.

---

* See the account of Father Menard, his mission and disappearance in the wilderness, etc. Neill's Hist. Minnesota, pp. 104 to 107 inc.

"Wakán-de!"* they answered his words, for he read from his book in the Latin,
Lest the Nazarene's holy commands by his tongue should be marred in translation;
And oft with his beads in his hands, or the cross and the crucified Jesus,
He knelt by himself on the sands, and his dim eyes uplifted to heaven.
But the braves bade him look to the East—to the silvery lodge of Han-nán-na;†
And to dance with the chiefs at the feast—at the feast of the Giant Heyó-ka.[16]
They frowned when the good father spurned the flesh of the dog in the kettle,
And laughed when his fingers were burned in the hot, boiling pot of the giant.
"The Black-robe" they called the poor priest, from the hue of his robe and his girdle;
And never a game or a feast but the father must grace with his presence.
His prayer-book the hunters revered,—they deemed it a marvelous spirit;
It spoke and the white father heard,—it interpreted visions and omens.
And often they bade him to pray this marvelous spirit to answer,
And tell where the sly Chippeway might be ambushed and slain in his forests.
For Menard was the first in the land, proclaiming, like John in the desert—
"The Kingdom of Heaven is at hand; repent ye, and turn from your idols."—
The first of the brave brotherhood that, threading the fens and the forest,
Stood afar by the turbulent flood at the falls of the Father of Waters.

In the lodge of the Stranger‡ he sat, awaiting the crown of a martyr;
His sad face compassion begat in the heart of the dark-eyed Winona.
Oft she came to the teepee and spoke; she brought him the tongue of the bison,
Sweet nuts from the hazel and oak, and flesh of the fawn and the mallard.
Soft hánpa§ she made for his feet and leggins of velvety fawn-skin,—
A blanket of beaver complete, and a hood of the hide of the otter.
And oft at his feet on the mat, deftly braiding the flags and the rushes,
Till the sun sought his teepee she sat, enchanted with what he related
Of the white-wingèd ships on the sea and the teepees far over the ocean,
Of the love and the sweet charity of the Christ and the beautiful Virgin.

She listened like one in a trance when he spoke of the brave, bearded Frenchmen,
From the green, sun-lit valleys of France to the wild Hochelága‖ transplanted,
Oft trailing the deserts of snow in the heart of the dense Huron forests,

---

*It is wonderful.
†The morning.
‡A lodge set apart for guests of the village.
§Moccasins.
‖The Ottawa name for the region of the St. Lawrence River.

Or steering the dauntless canoe through the waves of the fresh-water ocean.
"Yea, stronger and braver are they," said the aged Menard to Winona,
"Than the head-chief, tall Wazi-kuté,[4] but their words are as soft as a maiden's;
Their eyes are the eyes of the swan, but their hearts are the hearts of the eagles;
And the terrible Máza Wakán* ever walks by their side like a spirit.
Like a Thunder-bird, roaring in wrath, flinging fire from his terrible talons,
It sends to their enemies death, in the flash of the fatal Wakándee."†

The Autumn was past and the snow lay drifted and deep on the prairies;
From his teepee of ice came the foe—came the storm-breathing god of the winter.
Then roared in the groves,—on the plains,—on the ice-covered lakes and the river—
The blasts of the fierce hurricanes blown abroad from the breast of Wazíya.[3]
The bear cuddled down in his den, and the elk fled away to the forest;
The pheasant and gray prairie-hen made their beds in the heart of the snow-drift;
The bison-herds huddled and stood in the hollows and under the hill-sides,
Or rooted the snow for their food in the lee of the bluffs and the timber;
And the mad winds that howled from the north, from the ice-covered seas of Wazíya,
Chased the gray wolf and red fox and swarth to their dens in the hills of the forest.

Poor Father Menard,—he was ill; in his breast burned the fire of the fever;
All in vain was the magical skill of Wicásta Wakán[61] with his rattle;
Into soft, child-like slumber he fell, and awoke in the land of the blessèd—
To the holy applause of "Well done!" and the harps in the hands of the angels.
Long he carried the cross, and he won the coveted crown of a martyr.

In the land of the heathen he died, meekly following the voice of his Master,
One mourner alone by his side—Ta-té-psin's compassionate daughter.
She wailed the dead father with tears, and his bones by her kindred she buried.
Then winter followed winter. The years sprinkled frost on the head of her father;
And three weary winters she dreamed of the fearless and fair-bearded Frenchmen;
In her sweet sleep their swift paddles gleamed on the breast of the broad Mississippi,
And the eyes of the brave strangers beamed on the maid in the midst of her slumber.

She lacked not admirers; the light of the lover oft burned in her teepee—
At her couch in the midst of the night,—but she never extinguished the flambeau.

---

*"Mysterious metal"—or metal having a spirit in it. This is the common name applied by the Dakotas to all fire-arms.
†Lightning.

The son of Chief Wazi-kuté—a fearless and eagle-plumed warrior—
Long sighed for Winona, and he—was the pride of the band of Isántees.
Three times, in the night, at her bed, had the brave held the torch of the lover,[75]
And thrice had she covered her head and rejected the handsome Tamdóka.*

'Twas Summer.   The merry-voiced birds trilled and warbled in woodland and meadow;
And abroad on the prairies the herds cropped the grass in the land of the lilies,—
And sweet was the odor of rose wide-wafted from hillside and heather;
In the leaf-shaded lap of repose lay the bright, blue-eyed babes of the summer;
And low was the murmur of brooks, and low was the laugh of the Ha-Ha;[76]
And asleep in the eddies and nooks lay the broods of magá[60] and the mallard.
'Twas the moon of Wasúnpa.[71]   The band lay at rest in the tees at Ka-thá-ga,
And abroad o'er the beautiful land walked the spirits of Peace and of Plenty—
Twin sisters, with bountiful hand, wide scatt'ring wild-rice and the lilies.
An-pé-tu-wee[70] walked in the west—to his lodge in the midst of the mountains,
And the war-eagle flew to her nest in the oak on the Isle of the Spirit.†
And now at the end of the day, by the shore of the Beautiful Island,‡
A score of fair maidens and gay made joy in the midst of the waters.
Half-robed in their dark, flowing hair, and limbed like the fair Aphrodite,
They played in the waters, and there they dived and they swam like the beavers,—
Loud-laughing like loons on the lake when the moon is a round shield of silver,
And the songs of the whippowils wake on the shore in the midst of the maples.

But hark!—on the river a song,—strange voices commingled in chorus;
On the current a boat swept along with DuLuth and his hardy companions;
To the stroke of their paddles they sung, and this the refrain that they chanted:

"Dans mon chemin j'ai recontré
Deux cavaliers bien mouteés.
Lon, lon, laridon daine,
Lon, lon, laridon dai."

"Deux cavaliers bien mouteés;
L'un a cheval, et l'autre a pied.
Lon, lon, laridon daine,
Lon, lon, laridon dai."§

---

* Tah-mdo-kah—literally, the buck-deer.
†The Dakotas say that for many years in olden times a war-eagle made her nest in an oak-tree on Spirit-island—Wanagi-wita, just below the Falls, till frightened away by the advent of white men.
‡The Dakotas called Nicollet Island "Wi-ta Waste"—the Beautiful Island.
§A part of one of the favorite songs of the French *voyageurs*.

Like the red, dappled deer in the glade, alarmed by the footsteps of hunters,
Discovered, disordered, dismayed, the nude nymphs fled forth from the waters,
And scampered away to the shade, and peered from the screen of the lindens,

A bold and and adventuresome man was DuLuth, and a dauntless in danger,
And straight to Kathága he ran, and boldly advanced to the warriors,
Now gathering, a cloud, on the strand, and gazing amazed on the strangers;
And straightway he offered his hand unto Wázi-kuté, the Itáncan.
To the Lodge of the Stranger were led DuLuth and his hardy companions;
Robes of beaver and bison were spread, and the Peace-pipe[81] was smoked
    with the Frenchman.

There was dancing and feasting at night, and joy at the presents he lavished.
All the maidens were wild with delight with the flaming red robes and the ribbons,
With the beads and the trinkets untold, and the fair, bearded face of the giver;
And glad were they all to behold the friends from the Land of the Sunrise.
But one stood apart from the rest—the queenly and peerless Winona,
Intently regarding the guest—hardly heeding the robes and the ribbons,
Whom the White Chief beholding admired, and straightway he spread on her shoulders
A lily-red robe and attired, with necklet and ribbons, the maiden.
The red lilies bloomed in her face, and her glad eyes gave thanks to the giver,
And forth from her teepee apace she brought him the robe and the missal
Of the father—poor Renè Menard; and related the tale of the "Black Robe."
She spoke of the sacred regard he inspired in the hearts of Dakotas;
That she buried his bones with her kin, in the mound by the Cave of the Council;
That she treasured and wrapt in the skin of the red-deer his robe and his prayer-book—
"Till his brothers should come from the East—from the land of the far Hochelága,
To smoke with the braves at the feast, on the shores of the Loud-laughing Waters.[76]
For the "Black Robe" spake much of his youth and his friends in the Land
    of the Sunrise;
It was then as a dream; now in truth, I behold them, and not in a vision."
But more spake her blushes, I ween, and her eyes full of language unspoken,
As she turned with the grace of a queen, and carried her gifts to the teepee.

Far away from his beautiful France—from his home in the city of Lyons,
A noble youth full of romance, with a Norman heart big with adventure,
In the new world a wanderer, by chance, DuLuth sought the wild Huron forests.

But afar by the vale of the Rhone, the winding and musical river,
And the vine-covered hills of the Saône, the heart of the wanderer lingered,—
'Mid the vineyards and mulberry trees, and the fair fields of corn and of clover
That rippled and waved in the breeze, while the honey-bees hummed in the blossoms.
For there, where th' impetuous Rhone, leaping down from the Switzerland mountains,
And the silver-lipped, soft-flowing Saône, meeting, kiss and commingle together,
Down-winding by vineyards and leas, by the orchards of fig-trees and olives,
To the island-gemmed, sapphire-blue seas of the glorious Greeks and the Romans;
Aye, there, on the vine-covered shore, 'mid the mulberry-trees and the olives,
Dwelt his blue-eyed and beautiful Flore, with her hair like a wheat-field at harvest,
All rippled and tossed by the breeze, and her cheeks like the glow of the morning,
Far away o'er the emerald seas, ere the sun lifts his brow from the billows,
Or the red-clover fields when the bees, singing sipped the sweet cups of the blossoms.
Wherever he wandered—alone in the heart of the wild Huron forests,
Or cruising the rivers unknown to the land of the Crees or Dakotas—
His heart lingered still on the Rhone, 'mid the mulberry-trees and the vineyards,
Fast-fettered and bound by the zone that girdled the robes of his darling.

Till the red Harvest Moon[71] he remained in the vale of the swift Mississippi.
The esteem of the warriors he gained, and the love of the dark-eyed Winona.
He joined in the sports and the chase; with the hunters he followed the bison,
And swift were his feet in the race when the red elk they ran on the prairies.
At the Game of the Plum-stones[77] he played, and he won from the skillfulest players;
A feast to Wa'tánka he made, and he danced at the feast of Heyóka.[16]
With the flash and the roar of his gun he astonished the fearless Dakotas:
They called it the "Máza Wakán"—the mighty, mysterious metal.
"'Tis a brother," they said, "of the fire in the talons of dreadful Wakínyan,[32]
When he flaps his huge wings in his ire, and shoots his red shafts at Unktéhee."[60]

The Itáncan,[74] tall Wázi-kuté, appointed a day for the races.
From the red stake that stood by his tee, on the southerly side of the Ha-ha,
To a stake at the Lake of the Loons[79]—a league and return—was the distance.
On the crest of the hills red batoons marked the course for the feet of the runners.
They gathered from near and afar, to the races and dancing and feasting.
Five hundred tall warriors were there from Kapóza[6] and far-off Keóza;[4]

Kemnica,* too, furnished a share of the legions that thronged to the races.
And a bountiful feast was prepared by the diligent hands of the women,
And gaily the multitudes fared in the generous tees of Kathága.
The chief of the mystical clan appointed a feast to Unktéhee—
The mystic "Wacípee Wakán"†—at the end of the day and the races.
A band of sworn brothers are they, and the secrets of each one are sacred,
And death to the lips that betray is the doom of the swarthy avengers,
And the son of tall Wazí-kuté was the chief of the mystical order.

On an arm of an oak hangs the prize for the swiftest and strongest of runners—
A blanket as red as the skies, when the flames sweep the plains in October.
And beside it a strong, polished bow, and a quiver of iron-tipped arrows,
Which Kapóza's tall chief will bestow on the fleet-footed second that follows.
A score of swift-runners are there from the several bands of the nation;
And now for the race they prepare, and among them fleet-footed Tamdóka.
With the oil of the buck and the bear their sinewy limbs are anointed,
For fleet are the feet of the deer and strong are the limbs of the bruin,
And long is the course and severe for the swiftest and strongest of runners.

Hark!—the shouts and the braying of drums, and the Babel of tongues and confusion!
From his teepee the tall chieftain comes, and DuLuth brings a prize for the runners—
A keen hunting-knife from the Seine, horn-handled and mounted with silver.
The runners are ranged on the plain, and the Chief waves a flag as a signal,
And away like the gray wolves they fly—like the wolves on the trail of the red-deer;
O'er the hills and the prairie they vie, and strain their strong limbs to the utmost,
While high on the hills hangs a cloud of warriors and maidens and mothers,
To behold the swift-runners, and loud are the cheers and the shouts of the warriors.

Now swift from the lake they return, o'er the emerald hills and the heather;
Like grey-hounds they pant and they yearn, and the leader of all is Tamdóka.
At his heels flies Hu-pá-hu,‡ the fleet—the pride of the band of Kaóza,—
A warrior with eagled-winged feet, but his prize is the bow and the quiver.
Tamdóka first reaches the post, and his are the knife and the blanket,
By the mighty acclaim of the host and award of the chief and the judges.

---

*Pronounced Ray-mne-chah—The village of the Mountains, situate where Red Wing now stands.
†Sacred Dance—The Medicine-dance—See description infra.
‡The wings.

Then proud was the tall warrior's stride, and haughty his look and demeanor;
He boasted aloud in his pride, and he scoffed at the rest of the runners.
"Behold me, for I am a man!* my feet are as swift as the West-wind.
With the coons and the beavers I ran; but where is the elk or the cábri? [80]
Come!—where is the hunter will dare match his feet with the feet of Tamdóka?
Let him think of Taté † and beware, ere he stake his last robe on the trial."
"Ohó! Ho! Hó-héca!"‡ they jeered, for they liked not the boast of the boaster;
But to match him no warrior appeared, for his feet wore the wings of the west-wind.

Then forth from the side of the chief stepped DuLuth and he looked on the boaster;
"The words of a warrior are brief,—I will run with the brave," said the Frenchman;
"But the feet of Tamdóka are tired; abide till the cool of the sunset."
All the hunters and maidens admired, for strong were the limbs of the stranger.
"Hiwó! Ho!"§ they shouted and loud rose the cheers of the multitude mingled;
And there in the midst of the crowd stood the glad-eyed and blushing Winona.

Now afar o'er the plains of the west walked the sun at the end of his journey,
And forth came the brave and the guest, at the tap of the drum, for the trial.
Like a forest of larches the hordes were gathered to witness the contest;
As loud as the drums were their words and they roared like the roar of the Ha-ha.
For some for Tamdóka contend, and some for the fair, bearded stranger,
And the betting runs high to the end, with the skins of the bison and beaver.
A wife of tall Wazi-kuté—the mother of boastful Tamdóka—
Brought her handsomest robe from the tee, with a vaunting and loud proclamation:
She would stake her last robe on her son who, she boasted, was fleet as the Cábri, [80]
And the tall, tawny chieftain looked on, approving the boast of the mother.
Then fleet as the feet of a fawn to her lodge ran the dark-eyed Winona,
She brought and she staked on the lawn, by the side of the robe of the boaster,
The lily-red mantle DuLuth, with his own hands, had laid on her shoulders.
"Tamdóka is swift, but forsooth, the tongue of his mother is swifter,"
She said, and her face was aflame with the red of the rose and the lily,
And loud was the roar of acclaim; but dark was the face of Tamdóka.

---

*A favorite boast of the Dakota braves.   †The wind.
‡About equivalent to Oho!—Aha!—fudge!   §Hurra there!

They strip for the race and prepare,—DuLuth in his breeches and leggins;
And the brown, curling locks of his hair downward droop to his bare, brawny shoulders,
And his face wears a smile debonair, as he tightens his red sash around him;
But stripped to the moccasins bare, save the belt and the breech-clout of buckskin,
Stands the haughty Tamdóka aware that the eyes of the warriors admire him;
For his arms are the arms of a bear and his legs are the legs of a panther.

The drum beats,—the chief waves the flag, and away on the course speed the runners,
And away leads the brave like a stag,—like a hound on his track flies the Frenchman;
And away haste the hunters, once more, to the hills for a view to the lake-side,
And the dark-swarming hill-tops, they roar with the storm of loud voices commingled.
Far away o'er the prairie they fly, and still in the lead is Tamdóka,
But the feet of his rival are nigh, and slowly he gains on the hunter.
Now they turn on the post at the lake,—now they run full abreast on the home-stretch;
Side by side they contend for the stake, for a long mile or more on the prairie.
They strain like a stag and a hound, when the swift-river gleams through the thicket,
And the horns of the riders resound, winding shrill through the depths of the forest.
But behold!—at full length on the ground falls the fleet-footed Frenchman abruptly,
And away with a whoop and a bound, springs the eager, exulting Tamdóka.
Long and loud on the hills is the shout of his swarthy admirers and backers;
"But the race is not won till it 's out," said DuLuth, to himself as he gathered,
With a frown on his face, for the foot of the wily Tamdóka had tripped him.
Far ahead ran the brave on the route, and turning he boasted exultant.
Like spurs to the steed to DuLuth were the jeers and the taunts of the boaster;
Indignant was he and red wroth, at the trick of the runner dishonest;
And away like a whirlwind he speeds—like a hurricane mad from the mountains;
He gains on Tamdóka,—he leads!—and behold, with the spring of a panther,
He leaps to the goal and succeeds, 'mid the roar of the mad acclamation.

Then glad as the robin in May was the voice of Winona exulting;
And the crest-fallen brave turned away, and lonely he walked by the river;
He glowered as he went and the fire of revenge in his bosom was kindled,
But he strove to dissemble his ire, and he whistled alone by the Ha-ha.

THE "WAKAN-WACEPEE," OR SACRED DANCE.[1]

Lo the lights in the "Teepee Wakán!" 'tis the night of the Wakán-Wacépee.
Round and round walks the chief of the clan, as he rattles the sacred Ta-shá-kay;[1]
Long and loud on the Chán-che-ga[1] beat the drummers with magical drums icks,
And the notes of the Chó-tánka[1] greet, like the murmur of winds on the waters.
By the friction of white-cedar wood for the Feast was a Virgin-fire[20] kindled.
They that enter the firm brotherhood first must fast and be cleansed by E-neé-pee;[1]
And from foot-sole to crown of the head must they paint with the favorite colors;
For Unktéhee likes bands of blood-red, with the stripings of blue intermingled.
In the hollow earth, dark and profound, Unktéhee and fiery Wakin-yan
Long fought and the terrible sound of the battle was louder than thunder;
The mountains were heaved and around were scattered the hills and the boulders,
And the vast solid plains of the ground rose and fell like the waves of the ocean.
But the god of the waters prevailed. Wakin-yan escaped from the cavern,
And long on the mountains he wailed, and his hatred endureth forever.

When Unktéhee had finished the earth, and the beasts and the birds and the fishes,
And men at his bidding came forth from the heart of the huge hollow mountains[69]
A band chose the god from the hordes, and he said: "Ye are sons of Unktéhee:
Ye are lords of the beasts and the birds, and the fishes that swim in the waters.
But hearken ye now to my words,—let them sound in your bosoms forever:
Ye shall honor Unktéhee and hate Wakínyan, the Spirit of Thunder,
For the power of Untéhee is great, and he laughs at the darts of Wakínyan.
Ye shall honor the Earth and the Sun,--for they are your father and mother;[70]
Let your prayer to the Sun be:—*Wakán, Até; on-si-má-da oheé-neé.*"*
And remember the Táku Wakán,[73] all-pervading in earth and in ether—
Invisible ever to man, but he dwells in the midst of all matter;
Yea, he dwells in the heart of the stone--in the hard granite heart of the boulder;
Ye shall call him forever Tunkán—grandfather of all the Dakotas.
Ye are men that I choose for my own; ye shall be as a strong band of brothers,
Now I give you the magical bone and the magical pouch of the spirits.†
And these are the laws ye shall heed: Ye shall honor the pouch and the giver.

"Sacred Spirit! Father! have pity on me always."
†Riggs' Tahkoo Wakan, p. 90.

Ye shall walk as twin-brothers; in need, one shall forfeit his life for another.
Listen not to the voice of the crow.* Hold as sacred the wife of a brother.
Strike, and fear not the shaft of the foe, for the soul of the brave is immortal.
Slay the warrior in battle, but spare the innocent babe and the mother.
Remember a promise;—beware,—let the word of warrior be sacred.
When a stranger arrives at the tee—be he a friend of the band or foeman,
Give him food; let your bounty be free; lay a robe for the guest by the lodge-fire;
Let him go to his kindred in peace, if the peace-pipe he smoke in the teepee;
And so shall your children increase, and your lodges shall laugh with abundance.
And long shall ye live in the land, and the spirits of earth and the waters
Shall come to your aid, at command, with the power of invisible magic.
And at last, when you journey afar—o'er the shining "*Wanagee Ta-chan-ku,*" [65]
You shall walk as a red, shining star,[1] in the land of perpetual summer."

All the night in the teepee they sang, and they danced to the mighty Unktéhee,
While the loud-braying Chán-che-ga rang and the shrill-piping flute and the rattle,
Till Anpétuwee[66] rose in the east—from the couch of the blushing Han-nán-na,
And thus at the dance and the feast sang the sons of Unktéhee in chorus:

> "Wa-dú-ta o-hná mi-ká-ge!
> Wa-dú-ta o-hná mi-ká-ge!
> Mini-yàta ité wakándè makù,
> Atè wakán—Tunkánsidán,
>
> Tunkánsidán pejihúta wakán
> Micàgè—he Wicàgè!
> Miniyáta ité wakándé makú.
> Tankánsidan ite, nápè dú-win-ta woo,
> Wahutópa wan yúha, nápè dú-win-ta too."

TRANSLATION.

> In red swan-down he made it for me;
> In red swan-down he made it for me;
> He of the water—he of the mysterious face—
> Gave it to me;
> Sacred Father—Grandfather!

*Slander.

Grandfather made me magical medicine:
That is true!
Being of mystery,—grown in the water—
He gave it to me!
To the face of our Grandfather stretch out your hand;
Holding a quadruped, stretch out your hand!

Till high o'er the hills of the east Anpétuwee walked on his journey,
In secret they danced at the feast, and communed with the mighty Unktéhee.
Then opened the door of the tee to the eyes of the day and the people,
And the sons of Unktéhee, to be, were endowed with the sacred Ozúha,[82]
By the son of tall Wazí-kuté, Tamdôka, the chief of the Magi.
And thus since the birth-day of man—since he sprang from the heart of the mountains, [69]
Has the sacred "Wacépee Wakán" by the warlike Dakotas been honored,
And the god-favored sons of the clan work their will with the help of the spirits.

'Twas sunrise; the spirits of mist trailed their white robes on dewy savannas,
And the flowers raised their heads to be kissed by the first golden beams of the morning.
The breeze was abroad with the breath of the rose of the Isles of the Summer,
And the humming-bird hummed on the heath from his home in the land of the rain-bow.[*]
'Twas the morn of departure. DuLuth stood alone by the roar of the Ha-ha;
Tall and fair in the strength of his youth stood the blue-eyed and fair-bearded Frenchman.
A rustle of robes on the grass broke his dream as he mused by the waters,
And, turning, he looked on the face of Winona, wild rose of the prairies,
Half hid in her forest of hair, like the round, golden moon in the pine-tops.
Admiring he gazed—she was fair as his own blooming Flore in her orchards,
With her golden locks loose on the air, like the gleam of the sun through the olives,
Far away on the vine-covered shore, in the sun-favored land of his fathers.
"Lists the chief to the cataract's roar for the mournful lament of the Spirit?"[†]
Said Winona,—"The wail of the sprite, for her babe and its father unfaithful,
Is heard in the midst of the night, when the moon wanders dim in the heavens."

"Wild-Rose of the Prairies," he said, "DuLuth listens not to the Ha-ha,
For the wail of the ghost of the dead, for her babe and its father unfaithful;
But he lists to a voice in his heart that is heard by the ear of no other,
And to-day will the White Chief depart—he returns to the land of the sunrise."

_____

[*] The Dakotas say the humming-bird comes from the "land of the rain-bow."
[†] See Legend of the Falls, or Note 28—Appendix.

"Let Winona depart with the chief,—she will kindle the fire in his teepee ;
For long are the days of her grief, if she stay in the tee of Ta-té-psin,"
She replied. and her cheeks were aflame with the bloom of the wild prairie lilies.
"Tanké,* is the White Chief to blame?" said DuLuth to the blushing Winona.
"The White Chief is blameless," she said, "but the heart of Winona will follow
Wherever thy footsteps may lead, O blue-eyed brave Chief of the white men.
For her mother sleeps long in the mound, and a step-mother rules in the teepee,
And her father, once strong and renowned, is bent with the weight of his winters.
No longer he handles the spear,—no longer his swift, humming arrows
Overtake the fleet feet of the deer, or the bear of the woods, or the bison ;
But he bends as he walks, and the wind shakes his white hair and hinders his footsteps ;
And soon will he leave me behind, without brother or sister or kindred.
The doe scents the wolf in the wind, and a wolf walks the path of Winona.
Three times have the gifts for the bride[25] to the lodge of Ta-té-psin been carried,
But the voice of Winona replied that she liked not the haughty Tamdóka.
And thrice were the gifts sent away, but the tongue of the mother protested,
And the were-wolf[52] still follows his prey, and abides but the death of my father."

"I pity Winona," he said, "but my path is a pathway of danger,
And long is the trail for the maid to the far-away land of the sunrise ;
And few are the braves of my band, and the braves of Tamdóka are many ;
But soon I return to the land, and a cloud of my hunters will follow.
When the cold winds of winter return, and toss the white robes of the prairies,
The fire of the White Chief will burn in his lodge at the Meeting-of-Waters ;†
And when from the Sunrise again comes the chief of the sons of the Morning,
Many moons will his hunters remain in the land of the friendly Dakotas.
The son of Chief Wazi-Kuté guides the White Chief afar on his journey ;
Nor long on the Tonka Medé‡—on the breast of the blue, bounding billows—
Shall the bark of the Frenchman delay, but his pathway shall kindle behind him."

She was pale, and her hurried voice swelled with alarm as she questioned replying—
"Tamdóka thy guide?—I beheld thy death in his face, at the races !

*My Sister.

†Mendota—properly *Mdo-te*—meaning the out-let of a lake or river into another, commonly applied to the region about Fort Snelling.

‡Tonka Mede· Great Lake, i. e. Lake Superior. The Dakotas seem to have had no other name for it. They generally referred to it as *Mini-ya-ta—There at the water.*

He covers his heart with a smile, but revenge never sleeps in his bosom;
His tongue--it is soft to beguile; but beware of the pur of the panther!
For death, like a shadow, will walk by thy side in the midst of the forest,
Or follow thy path like a hawk on the trail of a wounded Mastinca.*
A son of Unktéhee is he,—the Chief of the crafty magicians;
They have plotted thy death; I foresee, and thy trail, it is red in the forest;
Beware of Tamdóka,—beware. Slumber not like the grouse of the woodlands,
With head under wing, for the glare of the eyes that sleep not are upon thee."

"Winona, fear not," said Duluth, "for I carry the fire of Wakínyan,†
And strong is the arm of my youth, and stout are the hearts of my warriors;
But Winona has spoken the truth, and the heart of the White Chief is thankful.
Hide this in thy bosom, dear maid,—'tis the crucified Christ of the white men.‡
Lift thy voice to his spirit in need, and his spirit will hear thee and answer;
For often he comes to my aid; he is stronger than all the Dakotas;
And the Spirits of evil, afraid, hide away when he looks from the heavens."
In her swelling, brown bosom she hid the crucified Jesus in silver;
"Wiwástè,"§ she sadly replied; in her low voice the rising tears trembled;
Her dewy eyes turned she aside, and she slowly returned to the teepees.
But still on the swift river's strand, admiring the graceful Winona,
As she gathered, with brown, dimpled hand, her hair from the wind, stood the Frenchman.

To bid the brave White Chief adieu, on the shady shore gathered the warriors;
His glad boatmen manned the canoe, and the oars in their hands were impatient.
Spake the Chief of Isántees,--"A feast will await the return of my brother
In peace rose the sun in the East, in peace in the West he descended.
May the feet of my brother be swift, till they bring him again to our teepees;
The red pipe he takes as a gift, may he smoke that red pipe many winters.
At my lodge-fire his pipe shall be lit, when the White Chief returns to Kathága;
On the robes of my tee shall he sit; he shall smoke with the chiefs of my people
The brave love the brave; and his son sends the Chief as a guide for his brother.
By the way of the Wákpa Wakán‖ to the Chief at the Lake of the Spirits.

---

*The rabbit. The Dakotas called the Crees "Mastineapi". Rabbits.
†I. e. a fire-arm, which the Dakotas compare to the roar of the wings of the Thunder-bird and the fiery arrows he shoots.
‡Duluth was a devout Catholic. §Nee-wahshtay—Thou art good.
‖Spirit-River, now called Rum River.

As light as the foot-steps of dawn are the feet of the stealthy Tamdóka,
And he fears not the Máza Wakán;* he is sly as the fox of the forest.
When he dances the dance of red war all the hungry wolves howl by the Big Sea,†
For they scent on the south-wind afar their feast on the bones of of Ojibways."
Thrice the Chief puffed the red pipe of peace, ere it passed to the lips of the Frenchman.
Spake DuLuth,—"May the Great Spirit bless with abundance the Chief and his people;
May their sons and their daughters increase, and the fire ever burn in their teepees."
Then he waved with a flag his adieu to the Chief and the warriors assembled;
And away shot Tamdóka's canoe to the strokes of ten sinewy hunters;
And a white path he clove up the blue, bubbling stream of the swift Mississippi;
And away on his foaming trail flew, like a sea-gull, the bark of the Frenchman.
Then merrily rose the blithe song of the *voyageurs* homeward returning,
And thus, as they glided along, sang the bugle-voiced boatmen in chorus:

SONG.

Home again! home again! bend to the oar!
Merry is the life of the gay *voyageur*.
He rides on the river with his paddle in his hand,
And his boat is his shelter on the water and the land.
The clam has his shell and the water-turtle too,
And the brave boatman's shell is his birch-bark canoe.
So pull away, boatmen; bend to the oar;
Merry is the life of the gay *voyageur*.

Home again! home again! bend to the oar!
Merry is the life of the gay *voyageur*.
His couch is as downy as a couch can be,
For he sleeps on the feathers of the green fir-tree.
He dines on the fat of the pemmican-sack,
And his *eau de vie* is the *eau de lac*.
So pull away, boatmen; bend to the oar;
Merry is the life of the gay *voyageur*.

Home again! home again! bend to the oar!
Merry is the life of the gay *voyageur*.

---

*Fire-arm—spirit-metal.
†Lake Superior—at that time the home of the Ojibways (Chippewas.)

5 *

The brave, jolly boatman,—he never is afraid
When he meets at the portage a red, forest maid,
A Huron, or a Cree, or a blooming Chippeway;
And he marks his trail with the *bois brulès.*
So pull away, boatmen; bend to the oar;
Merry is the life of the gay *voyageur.*
Home again! home again! bend to the oar!
Merry is the life of the gay *voyageur.*

In the reeds of the meadow the stag lifts his branchy head stately and listens,
And the bobolink, perched on the flag, her ear sidelong bends to the chorus.
From the brow of the Beautiful Isle,* half hid in the midst of the maples,
The sad-faced Winona, the while, watched the boat growing less in the distance.
Till away in the bend of stream, where it turned and was lost in the lindens,
She saw the last dip and the gleam of the oars ere they vanished forever.
Still afar on the waters the song, like bridal bells distantly chiming,
The stout, jolly boatmen prolong, beating time with the stroke of their paddles;
And Winona's ear, turned to the breeze, lists the air falling fainter and fainter.
Till it dies like the murmur of bees when the sun is aslant on the meadows.
Blow, breezes,—blow softly and sing in the dark, flowing hair of the maiden;
But never again shall you bring the voice that she loves to Winona.

Now a light, rustling wind from the South shakes his wings o'er the wide, wimpling waters;
Up the dark-winding river DuLuth follows fast in the wake of Tamdóka.
On the slopes of the emerald shores leafy woodlands and prairies alternate;
On the vine-tangled islands the flowers peep timidly out at the white men;
In the dark-winding eddy the loon sits warily watching and voiceless,
And the wild-goose, in reedy lagoon, stills the prattle and play of her children.
The does and their sleek, dappled fawns prick their ears and peer out from the thickets,
And the bison-calves play on the lawns, and gambol like colts in the clover.
Up the still-flowing Wákpa Wahán's winding path through the groves and the meadows,
Now DuLuth's brawny boatmen pursue the swift-gliding bark of Tamdóka ;
And hardly the red braves out-do the stout, steady oars of the white men.

Now they bend to their oars in the race—the ten tawny braves of Tamdóka ;
And hard on their heels in the chase ply the six stalwart oars of the Frenchmen.

'Wista Waste—Nicollet Island,

In the stern of his boat sits DuLuth; in the stern of his boat stands Tamdôka;
And warily, cheerily, both urge the oars of their men to the utmost.
Far-stretching away to the eyes, winding blue in the midst of the meadows,
As a necklet of sapphires that lies unclaspt in the lap of a virgin,
Here asleep in the lap of the plain lies the reed-bordered, beautiful river.
Like two flying coursers that strain, on the track, neck and neck, on the home-stretch,
With nostrils distended, and mane froth-flecked, and the neck and the shoulders,
Each urged to his best by the cry and the whip and the rein of his rider,
Now they skim o'er the waters and fly, side by side, neck and neck, through the meadows.
The blue heron flaps from the reeds, and away wings her course up the river;
Straight and swift is her flight o'er the meads, but she hardly outstrips the canoemen.
See! the *voyageurs* bend to their oars till the blue veins swell out on their foreheads;
And the sweat from their brawny breasts pours; but in vain their Herculean labor;
For the oars of Tamdôka are ten, and but six are the oars of the Frenchmen,
And the red warriors' burden of men is matched by the *voyageur's* luggage.
Side by side, neck and neck, for a mile, still they strain their strong arms to the utmost,
Till rounding a willowy isle, now ahead creeps the boat of Tamdôka,
And the neighboring forests profound, and the far-stretching plain of the meadows
To the whoop of the victors resound, while the panting French rest on their paddles.

With sable wings wide o'er the land, night sprinkles the dew of the heavens;
And hard by the dark river's strand, in the midst of a tall, somber forest,
Two camp-fires are lighted, and beam on the trunks and the arms of the pine trees.
In the fitful light darkle and gleam the swarthy-hued faces around them.
And one is the camp of DuLuth, and the other the camp of Tamdôka,
But few are the jests and uncouth of the *voyageurs* over their supper,
While moody and silent the braves round their fire in a circle sit crouching;
And low is the whisper of leaves and the sough of the wind in the branches;
And low is the long-winding howl of the lone wolf afar in the forest;
But shrill is the hoot of the owl, like a bugle-blast blown in the pine-tops,
And the half-startled *voyageurs* scowl at the sudden and saucy intruder.
Like the eyes of the wolves are the eyes of the watchful and silent Dakotas;
Like the face of the moon in the skies, when the clouds chase each other across it,
Is Tamdôka's dark face in the light of the flickering flames of the camp-fire.
They have plotted red murder by night, and securely contemplate their victims.
But wary and armed to the teeth are the resolute Frenchmen and ready,

If need be, to grapple with death, and to die hand to hand in the desert.
Yet skilled in the arts and the wiles of the cunning and crafty Algonkins,
They cover their hearts with their smiles, and hide their suspicions of evil.
Round their low, smouldering fire, feigning sleep, lie the watchful and wily Dakotas;
But DuLuth and his *voyageurs* heap their fire that shall blaze till the morning,
Ere they lay themselves snugly to rest, with their guns by their side on the blankets,
As if there were none to molest but the ravening beasts of the forest.

'Tis midnight.   The rising moon gleams, weird and still o'er the dusky horizon;
Through the hushed, somber forest she beams, and fitfully gloams on the meadows;
And a dim, glimmering pathway she paves, at times, on the dark stretch of river.
The winds are asleep in the caves—in the heart of the far-away mountains;
And here on the meadows and there, the lazy mists gather and hover;
And the lights of the Fen-Spirits[72] flare and dance on the low-lying marshes,
As still as the footsteps of death by the bed of the babe and its mother;
And hushed are the pines, and beneath lie the weary-limbed boatmen in slumber.
Walk softly,—walk softly, O Moon, through the gray, broken clouds in thy pathway,
For the earth lies asleep, and the boon of repose is bestowed on the weary.
Toiling hands have forgotten their care; e'en the brooks have forgotten to murmur;
But hark!—there's a sound on the air!—'tis the light-rustling robes of the Spirits.
Like the breath of the night in the leaves, or the murmur of reeds on the river,
In the cool of the mid-summer eves, when the blaze of the day has descended.
Low-crouching and shadowy forms, as still as the gray morning's footsteps,
Creep sly as the serpent that charms, on her nest in the meadow, the plover;
In the shadows of pine-trunks they creep, but their panther-eyes gleam in the fire-light,
As they peer on the white-men asleep, in the glow of the fire, on their blankets.
Lo, in each swarthy right-hand a knife; in the left-hand, the bow and the arrows!
Brave Frenchmen! awake to the strife!—or you sleep in the forest forever.
Nay, nearer and nearer they glide, like ghosts on the fields of their battles,
Till close on the sleepers, they bide but the signal of death from Tamdóka.
Still the sleepers sleep on.   Not a breath stirs the leaves of the awe-stricken forest;
The hushed air is heavy with death; like the footsteps of death are the moments.
"*Arise!*"—At the word, with a bound, to their feet spring the vigilant Frenchmen;
And the dark, dismal forests resound to the crack and the roar of their rifles;
And seven writhing forms on the ground clutch the earth.   From the pine-tops the
    screech-owl

Screams and flaps his wide wings in affright, and plunges away through the shadows;
And swift on the wings of the night flee the dim, phantom-forms of the spirits.
Like cabris[40] when white wolves pursue, fled the four yet-remaining Dakotas;
Through forest and fen-land they flew, and wild terror howled on their footsteps.
And one was Tamdôka.   DuLuth through the night sent his voice like a trumpet:
"Ye are Sons of Unktéhee, forsooth!   Return to your mothers, ye cowards!"
His shrill voice they heard as they fled, but only the echoes made answer.
At the feet of the brave Frenchmen, dead, lay seven swarthy Sons of Unktéhee;
And there, in the midst of the slain, they found, as it gleamed in the fire-light,
The horn-handled knife from the Seine, where it fell from the hand of Tamdôka.

THE UPPER WAKPA WAKAN OR SPIRIT RIVER.

In the gray of the morn, ere the sun peeped over the dewy horizon,
Their journey again was begun, and they toiled up the swift, winding river;
And many a shallow they passed on their way to the Lake of the Spirits;
But dauntless they reached it at last, and found Akee-pá-kee-tin's* village,
On an isle in the midst of the lake; and a day in his teepee they tarried.

Of the deed in the wilderness spake, to the brave Chief, the frank-hearted Frenchman.
A generous man was the Chief, and a friend of the fearless explorer;

*See Hennepin's account of "Aqui-pa-que-tin," and his village.   Shea's Hennepin, 225.

And dark was his visage with grief at the treacherous act of the warriors.
"Brave Wazi-Kuté is a man, and his heart is as clear as the sun-light;
But the head of a treacherous clan, and a snake-in-the-bush, is Tamdóka,"
Said the chief; and he promised DuLuth, on the word of a friend and a warrior,
To carry the pipe and the truth to his cousin, the chief at Kathága;
For thrice at the Tânka Medé had he smoked in the lodge of the Frenchman;
And thrice had he carried away the bountiful gifts of the trader.

When the chief could no longer prevail on the white men to rest in his teepee,
He guided their feet on the trail to the lakes of the winding Rice-River.*
Now on speeds the light bark canoe, through the lakes to the broad Gitchee Seebee;†
And up the great river they row,—up the Big Sandy Lake and Savanna;
And down through the meadows they go to the river of broad Gitchee Gumee.‡

DALLES OF THE ST. LOUIS.

Still onward they speed to the Dalles—to the roar of the white-rolling rapids,
Where the dark river tumbles and falls down the ragged ravine of the mountains,

* Now called "Mud River"—it empties into the Mississippi at Aitkin.
† Gitchee See-bee—Big River—is the Ojibway name for the Mississippi, which is a corruption of Gitchee Seebee—as Michigan is a corruption of Gitchee Gumee- Great Lake, the Ojibway name of Lake Superior.   ‡ The Ojibways call the St. Louis River Gitchee Gumee See-bee—Great-Lake River, i. e. the river of the Great Lake (Lake Superior).

And singing his wild jubilee to the low-moaning pines and the cedars,
Rushes on to the unsalted sea o'er the ledges upheaved by volcanoes.
Their luggage the *voyageurs* bore down the long, winding path of the portage,*
While they mingled their song with the roar of the turbid and turbulent waters.
Down-wimpling and murmuring there, twixt two dewy hills winds a streamlet,
Like a long, flaxen ringlet of hair on the breast of a maid in her slumber.

All safe at the foot of the trail, where they left it, they found their felucca,
And soon to the wind spread the sail, and glided at ease through the waters,—
Through the meadows and lakelets and forth, round the point stretching south
    like a finger,
From the mist-wreathen hill on the north, sloping down to the bay and the lake-side.
And behold, at the foot of the hill, a cluster of Chippewa wigwams,
And the busy wives plying with skill their nets in the emerald waters.
Two hundred white winters and more have fled from the face of the Summer
Since DuLuth, on that wild, somber shore, in the unbroken forest primeval,
From the midst of the spruce and the pines, saw the smoke of the wigwams up-curling,
Like the fumes from the temples and shrines of the Druids of old in their forests.
Ah, little he dreamed then, forsooth, that a city would stand on that hill-side,
And bear the proud name of DuLuth, the untiring and dauntless explorer,--
A refuge for ships from the storms, and for men from the bee-hives of Europe,
Out-stretching her long, iron arms o'er an empire of Saxons and Normans.

The swift west-wind sang in the sails, and on flew the boat like a sea-gull,
By the green, templed hills and the dales, and the dark rugged rocks of the North Shore;
For the course of the brave Frenchman lay to his fort at the Gáh-mah-na-ték-wáhk,[51]
By the shore of the grand Thunder Bay, where the gray rocks loom up into mountains;
Where the Stone Giant sleeps on the Cape, and the god of the storms'
    makes the thunder,[52]
And the Makinak[53] lifts his huge shape from 'he breast of the blue-rolling waters.
And thence to the south-westward led his course to the Holy Ghost Mission,[54]
Where the Black Robes, the brave shepherds, fed their wild sheep
    on the isle Wau-ga-bá-mé,[55]

---

*The route of DuLuth above described—from the mouth of the Wild-Rice (Mud) River, to Lake Superior—was for centuries and still is, the Indians' canoe-route. I have walked over the old portage from the foot of the Dalles to the St. Louis above—trod by the feet of half-breeds and *voyageurs* for more than two centuries, and by the Indians for, perhaps, a thousand years.

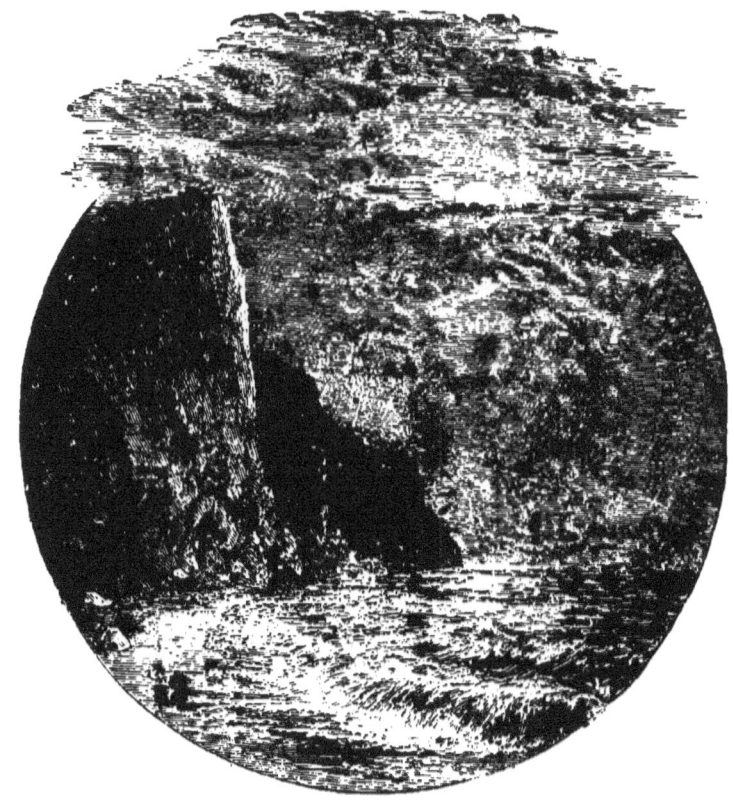

SUNSET BAY, LAKE SUPERIOR.

In the enchanting Cha-quám-e-gon Bay, defended by all the Apostles;*
And thence, by the Ke-we-naw, lay his course to the Mission Sainte Marie.†
Now the waves clap their myriad hands, and streams the white hair of the surges;
DuLuth at the steady helm stands, and he hums as he bounds o'er the billows:

> O sweet is the carol of bird,
> And sweet is the murmur of streams;
> But sweeter the voice that I heard—
> In the night—in the midst of my dreams.

*The Apostle Islands.   †At the Saut St. Marie.

'Tis the moon of the sere. falling leaves.   From the heads of the maples the west-wind
Plucks the red-and-gold plumage and grieves on the meads for the rose and the lily;
Their brown leaves the moaning oaks strew, and the breezes that roam on the prairies,
Low-whistling and wanton pursue the down of the silk-weed and thistle.
All sere are the prairies and brown, in the glimmer and haze of the Autumn;
From the far northern marshes flock down, by thousands, the geese and the mallards.
From the meadows and wide-prairied plains, for their long southward journey preparing,
In croaking flocks gather the cranes, and choose with loud clamor their leaders.
The breath of the evening is cold, and lurid along the horizon
The flames of the prairies are rolled, on the somber skies flashing their torches.
At noontide a shimmer of gold, through the haze. pours the sun from his pathway.
The wild-rice is gathered and ripe, on the moors, lie the scarlet po-pán-ka;*
Michábo'³ is smoking his pipe,—'tis the soft, dreamy Indian Summer,
When the god of the South⁹ as he flies from Waziya, the god of the Winter,
For a time turns his beautiful eyes, and backward looks over his shoulder.

It is noon.   From his path in the skies the red sun looks down on Kathága,
Asleep in the valley it lies, for the swift hunters follow the bison.
Ta-té-psin, the aged brave, bends as he walks by the side of Winona;
Her arm to his left hand she lends, and he feels with his staff for the pathway;
On his slow, feeble footsteps attends his gray dog, the watchful Wicháka;†
For blind in his years is the chief of a fever that followed the Summer,
And the days of Ta-té-psin are brief.   Once more by the dark-rolling river
Sits the Chief in the warm, dreary haze of the beautiful Summer in Autumn;
And the faithful dog lovingly lays his head at the feet of his master.
On a dead, withered branch sits a crow, down-peering askance at the old man;
On the marge of the river below romp the nut-brown and merry-voiced children,
And the dark waters silently flow, broad and deep, to the plunge of the Ha-Ha.

By his side sat Winona.   He laid his thin, shriveled hand on her tresses.
"Winona, my daughter," he said, "no longer thy father beholds thee ;
But he feels the long locks of thy hair, and the days that are gone are remembered.
When Sisóka‡ sat faithful and fair in the lodge of swift-footed Ta-té-psin.
The white years have broken my spear; from my bow they have taken the bow-string;

'Cranberries.   †Wee-chah-kah—literally "Faithful."
‡The Robin—the name of Winona's Mother.

But once on the trail of the deer, like a gray wolf from sunrise till sunset,
By woodland and meadow and mere, ran the feet of Ta-té-psin untiring.
But dim are the days that are gone, and darkly around me they wander,
Like the pale, misty face of the moon when she walks through the storm of the winter;
And sadly they speak in my ear. I have looked on the graves of my kindred.
The Land of the Spirits is near. Death walks by my side like a shadow.
Now open thine ear to my voice, and thy heart to the wish of thy father,
And long will Winona rejoice that she heeded the words of Ta-té-psin.
The cold, cruel winter is near, and famine will sit in the teepee.
What hunter will bring me the deer, or the flesh of the bear or the bison?
For my kinsmen before me have gone; they hunt in the land of the shadows.
In my old age forsaken, alone, must I die in my tecpee of hunger?
Winona, Tamdóka can make my empty lodge laugh with abundance;
For thine aged and blind father's sake, to the son of the Chief speak the promise:
For gladly again to my tee will the bridal gifts come for my daughter.
A fleet-footed hunter is he, and the good spirits feather his arrows;
And the cold, cruel winter will be a feast-time instead of a famine."

"My father," she said, and her voice was filial and full of compassion,
"Would the heart of Ta-té-psin rejoice at the death of Winona, his daughter?
The crafty Tamdóka I hate. Must I die in his teepee of sorrow?
For I love the White Chief, and I wait his return to the land of Dakotas.
When the cold winds of winter return, and toss the white robes of the prairies,
The fire of the White Chief will burn, in his lodge, at the Meeting-of-Waters.
Winona's heart followed his feet far away to the land of the morning,
And she hears in her slumber his sweet, kindly voice call the name of thy daughter.
My father, abide, I entreat, the return of the brave to Kathága.
The wild-rice is gathered, the meat of the bison is stored in the teepee:
Till the Coon-Moon[7] enough and to spare; and if then the white warrior return not,
Winona will follow the bear, and the coon, to their dens in the forest.
She is strong; she can handle the spear; she can bend the stout bow of the hunter;
And swift on the trail of the deer will she run o'er the snow on her snow-shoes.
Let the step-mother sit in the tee, and kindle the fire for my father;
And the cold, cruel winter shall be a feast-time instead of a famine."
"The White Chief will never return," half angrily muttered Ta-té-psin;
His camp-fire will nevermore burn in the land of the warriors he slaughtered.

I grieve, for my daughter has said that she loves the false friend of her kindred;
For the hands of the White Chief are red with the blood of the trustful Dakotas."
Then warmly Winona replied, "Tamdóka himself is the traitor,
And the white-hearted stranger had died by his treacherous hand in the forest,
But thy daughter's voice bade him beware of the sly death that followed his footsteps.
The words of Tamdóka are fair, but his heart is the den of the serpents.
When the braves told their tale, like a bird sang the heart of Winona rejoicing,
But gladlier still had she heard of the death of the crafty Tamdóka.
The Chief will return; he is bold, and he carries the fire of Wakínyan:
To our people the truth will be told, and Tamdóka will hide like a coward."
His thin locks the aged brave shook; to himself half-inaudibly muttered;
To Winona no answer he spoke—only moaned he "Micúnksee! Micúnksee!*
In my old age forsaken and blind! Yun! Hé-hé! Micúnksee! Micúnksee!"†
And Wicháka, the pitying dog, whined, as he looked on the face of his master.

Wazíya came down from the North—from his land of perpetual winter.
From his frost-covered beard issued forth the sharp-biting, shrill-whistling North-wind;
At the touch of his breath the wide earth turned to stone, and the lakes and the rivers;
From his nostrils the white vapors rose, and they covered the sky like a blanket.
Like the down of Magá‡ fell the snows, tossed and whirled into heaps by the North-wind.
Then the blinding storms roared on the plains, like the simoons on sandy Sahara;
From the fangs of the fierce hurricanes fled the elk and the deer and the bison.
Ever colder and colder it grew, till the frozen earth cracked and split open;
And harder and harder it blew, till the prairies were bare as the boulders.
To the southward the buffaloes fled, and the white rabbits hid in their burrows;
On the bare sacred mounds of the dead howled the gaunt, hungry wolves in the night-time.
The strong hunters crouched in their tees; by the lodge-fires the little ones shivered;
And the Magic-Men§ danced to appease, in their teepee, the wrath of Wazíya;
But famine and fatal disease, like phantoms, crept into the village.
The Hard Moon‖ was past, but the moon when the coons make their trails in the forest¶
Grew colder and colder. The coon, or the bear, ventured not from his cover;
For the cold, cruel Arctic Simoon swept the earth like the breath of a furnace.
In the tee of Ta-té-psin the store of wild-rice and dried meat was exhausted;
And Famine crept in at the door, and sat crouching and gaunt by the lodge-fire.

*My Daughter; My Daughter!   †Alas, O My Daughter,—My Daughter!
‡Wild-goose.   §Medicine-men.   ‖January.   ¶February.

But now with the saddle of deer, and the gifts, came the crafty Tamdóka;

And he said, "Lo I bring you good cheer, for I love the blind Chief and his daughter.

Take the gifts of Tamdóka, for dear to his heart is the dark-eyed Winona."

The aged Chief opened his ears; in his heart he already consented;

But the moans of his child and her tears touched the age-softened heart of the father,

And he said, "I am burdened with years,—I am bent by the snows of my winters;

Ta-té-psin will die in his tee; let him pass to the Land of the Spirits;

But Winona is young; she is free, and her own heart shall choose her a husband."

The dark warrior strode from the tee; low-muttering and grim he departed.

"Let him die in his lodge," muttered he, "but Winona shall kindle my lodge-fire."

Then forth went Winona. The bow of Ta-té-psin she took and his arrows,

And afar o'er the deep, drifted snow, through the forest, she sped on her snow-shoes.

Over meadow and ice-covered mere, through the thickets of red-oak and hazel,

She followed the tracks of the deer, but like phantoms they fled from her vision.

From sunrise till sunset she sped; half-famished she camped in the thicket;

In the cold snow she made her lone bed ; on the buds of the birch* made her supper.

To the dim moon the gray owl preferred, from the tree-top, his shrill lamentation,

And around her at midnight she heard the dread famine-cries of the gray wolves.

In the gloam of the morning again on the trail of the red-deer she followed—

All day long through the thickets in vain, for the gray wolves were chasing the roebucks;

And the cold, hungry winds from the plain chased the wolves and the deer and Winona.

In the twilight of sundown she sat, in the forest, all weak and despairing;

Ta-té-psin's bow lay at her feet, and his otter-skin quiver of arrows.

"He promised,—he promised," she said,—half-dreamily uttered and mournful,—

"And why comes he not? Is he dead? Was he slain by the crafty Tamdóka?

Must Winona, alas, make her choice—make her choice between death and Tamdóka?

She will die, but her soul will rejoice in the far Summer-land of the spirits.

Hark! I hear his low, musical voice! He is coming! My White Chief is coming!

Ah, no; I am half in a dream!—'twas the mem'ry of days long departed;

But the birds of the green Summer seem to be singing above in the branches."

Then forth from her bosom she drew the crucified Jesus in silver.

In her dark hair the cold north-wind blew, as meekly she bent o'er the image.

"O Christ of the White man," she prayed, "lead the feet of my brave to Kathága;

---

* The pheasant feeds on birch-buds in winter. Indians eat them when very hungry.

Send a good spirit down to my aid, or the friend of the White Chief will perish."
Then a smile on her wan features played, and she lifted her pale face and chanted:

> "E-ye-he-ktá! E-ye-he-ktá!
> Hé-kta-cè; é-ye-ce-quón.
> Mí-Wamdee-ská, he-he-ktá;
> He-kta-cè; é-ye-ce-quón,
> Mí-Wamdee-ská."

[TRANSLATION.]

> He will come; he will come;
> He will come, for he promised.
> My White Eagle, he will come;
> He will come, for he promised,—
> My White Eagle.

Thus sadly she chanted, and lo—allured by her sorrowful accents—
From the dark covert crept a red doe and wondrously gazed on Winona.
Then swift caught the huntress her bow; from her trembling hand hummed
the keen arrow.
Up-leaped the red gazer and fled, but the white snow was sprinkled with scarlet,
And she fell in the oak thicket dead. On the trail ran the eager Winona.
Half-famished the raw flesh she ate. To the hungry maid sweet was her supper.
Then swift through the night ran her feet, and she trailed the sleek red-deer behind her.
And the guide of her steps was a star—the cold-glinting star of Waziya—*
Over meadow and hilltop afar, on the way to the lodge of her father.
But hark! on the keen frosty air wind the shrill hunger-howls of the gray wolves!
And nearer,—still nearer!—the blood of the doe have they scented and follow;
Through the thicket, the meadow, the wood, dash the pack on the trail of Winona.
Swift she speeds with her burden, but swift on her track fly the minions of famine;
Now they yell on the view from the drift, in the reeds at the marge of the meadow;
Red gleam their wild, ravenous eyes; for they see on the hill-side their supper;
The dark forest echoes their cries; but her heart is the heart of a warrior.
From its sheath snatched Winona her knife, and a leg from the red doe she severed;
With the carcass she ran for her life,—to a low-branching oak ran the maiden;
Round the deer's neck her head-strap† was tied; swiftly she sprang to the arms of the
oak-tree;

---

*Waziya's Star is the North-star.   †A strap used in carrying burdens.

Quick her burden she drew to her side, and higher she clomb on the branches,
While the maddened wolves battled and bled, dealing death o'er the leg to each other;
Their keen fangs devouring the dead,—yea, devouring the flesh of the living,
They raved and they gnashed and they growled, like the fiends in the regions infernal;
The wide night re-echoing howled, and the hoarse North-wind laughed o'er the slaughter.
But their ravenous maws unappeased by the blood and the flesh of their fellows,
To the cold wind their muzzles they raised, and the trail to the oak-tree they followed.
Round and round it they howled for the prey, madly leaping and snarling and snapping;
But the brave maiden's keen arrows slay, till the dead number more than the living.
All the long, dreary night-time, at bay, in the oak sat the shivering Winona;
But the sun gleamed at last, and away skulked the gray cowards* down through the forest.
Then down dropped the doe and the maid. Ere the sun reached the midst of his journey,
Her red, welcome burden she laid at the feet of her famishing father.

Waziya's wild wrath was appeased, and homeward he turned to his teepee,¹
O'er the plains and the forest-land breezed, from the Islands of Summer, the South-wind.
From their dens came the coon and the bear; o'er the snow through the woodlands they
    wandered;
On her snow-shoes with stout bow and spear on their trails ran the huntress Winona.
The coon to his den in the tree, and the bear to his burrow she followed;
A brave, skillful hunter was she, and Ma-té-psin's lodge laughed with abundance.

The long winter wanes. On the wings of the spring come the geese and the mallards;
On the bare oak the red-robin sings, and the crocuses peep on the prairies,
And the bobolink pipes, but he brings, of the blue-eyed, brave White Chief, no tidings.
With the waning of winter, alas, waned the life of the aged Tatépsin;
Ere the blue pansies peeped from the grass, to the Land of the Spirits he journeyed;
Like a babe in its slumber he passed, or the snow from the hill-tops in April;
And the dark-eyed Winona, at last, stood alone by the graves of her kindred.
When their myriad mouths opened the trees to the sweet dew of heaven and the rain drops,
And the April showers fell on the leas, on his mound fell the tears of Winona.
Round her drooping form gathered the years and the spirits unseen of her kindred,
As low, in the midst of her tears, at the grave of her father she chanted:

---

*Wolves sometimes attack people at night, but rarely, if ever, in the day time. If they have followed
a hunter all night, or "treed" him, they will skulk away as soon as the sun rises.

E-yó-tan-han e-yáy-wah-ké-yày!
E-yó-tan-han e-yáy-wah-ké-yày!
E-yó-tan-han e-yáy-wah-ké-yày!
Ma-káh kin háy-chay-dan táy-han wan-kày.
Tú-way ne ktáy snee e-yáy-chen e-wáh chày.
E-yó-tan-han e-yáy-wah-ké-yày!
E-yó-tan-han e-yáy-wah-ké-yày!
Ma-káh kin háy-chay-dan táy-han wan-kày.

[TRANSLATION].

Sore is my sorrow!
Sore is my sorrow!
Sore is my sorrow!
The earth alone lasts.
I speak as one dying;
Sore is my sorrow!
Sore is my sorrow!
The earth alone lasts.

Still hope, like a star in the night gleaming oft through the broken clouds somber,
Cheered the heart of Winona, and bright, on her dreams, beamed the face
      of the Frenchman.
As the thought of a loved one and lost, sad and sweet were her thoughts
      of the White Chief;
In the moon's mellow light, like a ghost, walked Winona alone by the Ha-ha,
Ever wrapped in a dream. Far away—to the land of the sunrise—she wandered;
On the blue-rolling Tánka Medé,* in the midst of her dreams, she beheld him—
In his white-winged canoe, like a bird, to the land of Dakotas returning;
And often in fancy she heard the dip of his oars on the river.
On the dark waters glimmered the moon, but she saw not the boat of the Frenchman;
On the somber night bugled the loon, but she heard not the song of the boatmen.
The moon waxed and waned, but the star of her hope never waned to the setting;
Through her tears she beheld it afar, like a torch on the eastern horizon.
"He will come,—he is coming," she said; "he will come, for my White Eagle promised,"
And low to the bare earth the maid bent her ear for the sound of his footsteps.
"He is gone, but his voice in my ear still remains like the voice of the robin;
He is far, but his footsteps I hear; he is coming; my White Chief is coming!"

* Lake Superior,—The *Gitchee Gumee* of the Chippewas.

But the moon waxed and waned. Nevermore will the eyes of Winona behold him
Far away on the dark, rugged shore of the blue Gitchee Gúmee he lingers.
No tidings the rising sun brings; no tidings the star of the evening;
But morning and evening she sings, like a turtle-dove widowed and waiting:

Aké u, aké u, aké u;	Come again, come again, come again;
Ma cánté maséca.	For my heart is sad.
Aké u, aké u, aké u;	Come again, come again, come again;
Ma cánté maséca.	For my heart is sad.

Down the broad Gitchee Seebee* the band took their way to the Games at Keóza,*
While the swift-footed hunters by land ran the shores for the elk and the bison.
Like magás† ride the birchen canoes on the breast of the dark Gitchee Seebee;
By the willow-fringed islands they cruise, by the grassy hills green to their summits;
By the lofty bluffs hooded with oaks that darken the deep with their shadows;
And bright in the sun gleam the strokes of the oars in the hands of the women.
With the band went Winona.   The oar plied the maid with the skill of a hunter.
They loitered and camped on the shore of Remnica—the Lake of the Mountains.‡
There the fleet hunters followed the deer, and the thorny *pahin§* for the women.
From the tees rose the smoke of good cheer, curling blue through the tops of the maples,
Near the foot of a cliff that arose, like the battle-scarred walls of a castle.
Up-towering, in rugged repose, to a dizzy height over the waters.

But the man-wolf still followed his prey, and the step-mother ruled in the teepee;
Her will must Winona obey, by the custom and law of Dakotas.
The gifts to the teepee were brought—the blankets and beads of the White men,
And Winona, the orphaned, was bought by the crafty, relentless Tamdóka.
In the Spring-time of life, in the flush of the gladsome mid-May days of Summer,
When the bobolink sang and the thrush, and the red robin chirped in the branches,
To the tent of the brave must she go; she must kindle the fire in his teepee;
She must sit in the lodge of her foe, as a slave at the feet of her master.
Alas for her waiting! the wings of the East-wind have brought her no tidings;
On the meadow the meadow-lark sings, but sad is her song to Winona,
For the glad warbler's melody brings but the memory of voices departed.

---

* Chippewa name of the Mississippi.
† Wild Geese.
‡ Lake Pepin: by Hennepin called Lake of Tears—Called by the Dakotas Remnee-chah-Mday—Lake of the Mountains.
§ Pah-hin—the porcupine—the quills of which are greatly prized for ornamental work.

The Day-Spirit walked in the west to his lodge in the land of the shadows;
His shining face gleamed on the crest of the oak-hooded hills and the mountains,
And the meadow-lark hied to her nest, and the mottled owl peeped from her cover.
But hark! from the teepees a cry! Hear the shouts of the hurrying warriors!
Are the steps of the enemy nigh,—of the crafty and creeping Ojibways?
Nay; look on the dizzy cliff high!—on the brink of the cliff stands Winona!
Her sad face up-turned to the sky. Hark! I hear the wild chant of her death-song:

My Father's Spirit, look down, look down—
From your hunting-grounds in the shining skies;
Behold, for the light of my soul is gone.—
The light is gone and Winona dies.

I looked to the East, but I saw no star;
The face of my White Chief was turned away.
I harked for his footsteps in vain; afar
His bark sailed over the Sunrise-sea.

Long have I watched till my heart is cold;
In my breast it is heavy and cold as stone.
No more shall Winona his face behold,
And the robin that sang in her heart is gone.

Shall I sit at the feet of the treacherous brave?
On his hateful couch shall Winona lie?
Shall she kindle his fire like a coward slave?
No!—a warrior's daughter can bravely die.

My Father's Spirit, look down, look down—
From your hunting-grounds in the shining skies;
Behold, for the light of my soul is gone.—
The light is gone and Winona dies.

Swift the strong hunters clomb as she sang, and the foremost of all was Tamdóka;
From crag to crag upward he sprang; like a panther he leaped to the summit.
Too late! on the brave as he crept turned the maid in her scorn and defiance;
Then swift from the dizzy height leaped. Like a brant arrow-pierced in mid-heaven,
Down-whirling and fluttering she fell, and headlong plunged into the waters.
Forever she sank mid the wail, and the wild lamentation of women.
Her lone spirit evermore dwells in the depths of the Lake of the Mountains,
And the lofty cliff evermore tells to the years as they pass her sad story.*

* The Dakotas say that the spirit of Winona forever haunts the lake. They say that it was many, many winters ago when Winona leaped from the rock—that the rock was then perpendicular to the water's edge and she leaped into the lake, but now the rock has worn away, or the water has receded, so that it does not reach the foot of the rock.

In the silence of sorrow the night o'er the earth spread her wide, sable pinions;
And the stars [18] hid their faces; and light on the lake fell the tears of the spirits.
As her sad sisters watched on the shore for her spirit to rise from the waters,
They heard the swift dip of an oar, and a boat they beheld like a shadow,
Gliding down through the night in the gray, gloaming mists on the face of the waters.
'Twas the bark of DuLuth on his way from the Falls to the Games at Keóza.

" DOWN THE RAGGED RAVINE OF THE MOUNTAINS." DALLES OF THE ST. LOUIS.

THE LEGEND OF THE FALLS.*

[Read at the celebration of the Old Settlers of Hennepin County, at the Academy of Music, Minneapolis, July 4, 1879.]

(The numerals refer to notes in the Appendix.)

On the Spirit-Island† sitting under midnight's misty moon,
Lo I see the spirits flitting o'er the waters one by one!
Slumber wraps the silent city, and the droning mills are dumb;
One lone whippowil's shrill ditty calls her mate that ne'er will come.
Sadly moans the mighty river, foaming down the fettered falls,
Where of old he thundered ever o'er abrupt and lofty walls.
Great Unktèhee[60]—god of waters—lifts no more his mighty head;—
Fled he with the timid otters?—lies he in the cavern dead?

Hark!—the waters hush their sighing, and the whippowil her call,
Through the moon-lit mists are flying dusky shadows silent all.
Lo from out the waters foaming—from the cavern deep and dread—
Through the glamour and the gloaming, comes a spirit of the dead.
Sad she seems; her tresses raven on her tawny shoulders rest;
Sorrow on her brow is graven, in her arms a babe is pressed.
Hark!—she chants the solemn story,—sings the legend sad and old,
And the river wrapt in glory listens while the tale is told.

---

*An-pe-tu Sa-pa—Clouded Day—was the name of the Dakota mother who committed suicide, as related in this legend, by plunging over the Falls of St. Anthony. Schoolcraft calls her "*Ampata* Sapa." *Ampata* is not Dakota. There are several versions of this legend, all agreeing in the main points.

†The small island of rock a few rods below the Falls, was called by the Dakotas Wanagee We-ta—Spirit-Island. They say the spirit of Anpetu Sapa sits upon that island at night and pours forth her sorrow in song. They also say that from time out of mind, war-eagles nested on that island, until the advent of white men frightened them away. This seems to be true. Carver's Travels [London 1778], p. 7 1

Would you hear the legend olden, hearken while I tell the tale—
Shorn, alas, of many a golden, weird Dakota chant and wail.

THE LEGEND.

Tall was young Wanâta, stronger than Heyóka's[16] giant form,—
Laughed at flood and fire and hunger, faced the fiercest winter storm.
When Wakínyan[12] flashed and thundered, when Unktéhee raved and roared,
All but brave Wanâta wondered, and the gods with fear implored.
When the war-whoop wild resounded, calling friends to meet the foe,
From the teepee swift he bounded, armed with polished lance and bow.
In the battle's din and clangor fast his fatal arrows flew,
Flashed his fiery eyes with anger,—many a haughty foe he slew.
Hunter, swift was he and cunning, caught the beaver, slew the bear,
Overtook the roebuck running, dragged the panther from his lair.
Loved was he by many a maiden; many a dark eye glanced in vain;
Many a heart with sighs was laden for the love it might not gain.
So they called the brave "Ska Câpa";* but the fairest of the band—
Moon-faced, meek Anpétu-Sâpa—won the hunter's heart and hand.

From the wars with triumph burning, from the chase of bison fleet,
To his lodge the brave returning, spread his trophies at her feet.
Love and joy sat in the teepee; him a black-eyed boy she bore;
But alas, she lived to weep a love she lost forevermore.
For the warriors chose Wanâta first Itâncan† of the band.
At the council-fire he sat a leader loved a chieftain grand.
Proud was fair Anpétu-Sâpa, and her eyes were glad with joy;
Proud was she and very happy, with her chieftain and her boy.
But alas, the fatal honor that her brave Wanâta won,
Brought a bitter woe upon her,—hid with clouds the summer sun.

---

*Or Capa Ska—White beaver. White beavers are very rare, very cunning and hard to catch.
†E-tan-can—Chief.

For among the brave Dakotas, wives bring honor to the chief.
On the vine-clad Minnesota's banks he met the Scarlet Leaf.
Young and fair was Apè-dúta*—full of craft and very fair;
Proud she walked a queen of beauty with her wondrous flowing hair.
In her net of hair she caught him—caught Wanâta with her wiles;
All in vain his wife besought him—begged in vain his wonted smiles.
Apè-dúta ruled the teepee—all Wanâta's smiles were hers;   •
When the lodge was wrapped in sleep a start beheld the mother's tears.
Long she strove to do her duty for the black-eyed babe she bore;
But the proud, imperious beauty made her sad forevermore.
Still she dressed the skins of beaver, bore the burdens, spread the fare;
Patient ever, murmuring never, while her cheeks were creased with care.

In the moon Magâ-o-Kâda,[n] twice an hundred years ago—
Ere the "Black Robe's"‡ sacred shadow stalked the prairies' pathless snow—
Down the swollen, rushing river, in the sunset's golden hues,
From the hunt of bear and beaver came the band in swift canoes.
On the queen of fairy islands, on the Wita-Wâstè's§ shore,
Camped Wanâta, on the highlands, just above the cataract's roar.
Many braves were with Wanâta: Apè-dúta, too, was there,
And the sad Anpétu-sâpa spread the lodge with wonted care.
Then above the leafless prairie leaped the fat-faced, laughing moon,
And the stars—the spirits fairy—walked the welkin one by one.
Swift and silent in the gloaming on the waste of waters blue,
Speeding downward to the foaming, shot Wanâta's birch canoe,
In it stood Anpétu-sâpa—in her arms her sleeping child;
Like a wailing Norse-land *drapa*¶ rose her death-song weird and wild:

---

* Stars, the Dakotas say, are the faces of departed friends watching over their friends and relatives on earth.
† The Dakotas called the Jesuit priests "Black Robes" from the color of their vestments.
‡ Wee-tah Wah-stay—Beautiful Island,—the Dakota name for Nicollet Island, just above the Falls.
§ A-pe—leaf,—duta—Scarlet,—Scarlet leaf.
¶ *Drapa*, a Norse funeral wail in which the virtues of the deceased are recounted.

Mihihna,* Mihihna, my heart is stone;
The light is gone from my longing eyes;
The wounded loon in the lake alone
Her death-song sings to the moon and dies.

Mihihna, Mihihna, the path is long,
The burden is heavy and hard to bear;
I sink,—I die, and my dying song
Is a song of joy to the false one's ear.

Mihihna, Mihihna, my young heart flew
Far away with my brave to the bison-chase;
To the battle it went with my warrior true,
And never returned till I saw his face.

Mihihna, Mihihna, my brave was glad
When he came from the chase of the roebuck fleet;
Sweet were the words that my hunter said,
As his trophies he laid at Anpétu's feet.

Mihihna, Mihihna, the boy I bore—
When the robin sang and my brave was true,
I can bear to look on his face no more,
For he looks, Mihihna, so much like you.

Mihihna, Mihihna, the Scarlet Leaf
Has robbed my boy of his father's love;
He sleeps in my arms—he will find no grief
In the star-lit lodge in the land above.

Mihihna, Mihihna, my heart is stone,
The light is gone from my longing eyes;
The wounded loon in the lake alone,
Her death-song sings to the moon and dies.

Swiftly down the turbid torrent, as she sung her song she flew:
Like a swan upon the current, dancing rode the light canoe.
Hunters hurry in the gloaming, all in vain Wanâta calls;
Singing through the surges foaming, lo she plunges o'er the Falls.

---

*Mee-heen-yah—My husband

Long they search the sullen river—searched for leagues along the shore,
Bark or babe or mother never saw the sad Dakotas more;
But at night or misty morning oft the hunters heard her song,
Oft the maidens heard her warning in their mellow mother-tongue.

On the bluffs they sat enchanted till the blush of beamy dawn;
Spirit-Isle, they say, is haunted, and they call the spot "Wakân."*
Many summers on the highland, in the full-moon's golden glow—
In the woods on Fairy Island,† walked a snow white fawn and doe—
Spirits of the babe and mother sadly seeking evermore,
For a father's love another turned with evil charm and power.

Sometimes still when moonbeams shimmer through the maples on the lawn,
In the gloaming and the glimmer walk the silent doe and fawn;
And on Spirit-Isle or near it, under midnight's misty moon,
Oft is seen the mother's spirit, oft is heard her mournful tune.

*Pronounced Walk-on,—Sacred, inhabited by a Spirit.
†Fairy Island,—Wita Waste—Nicollet Island.

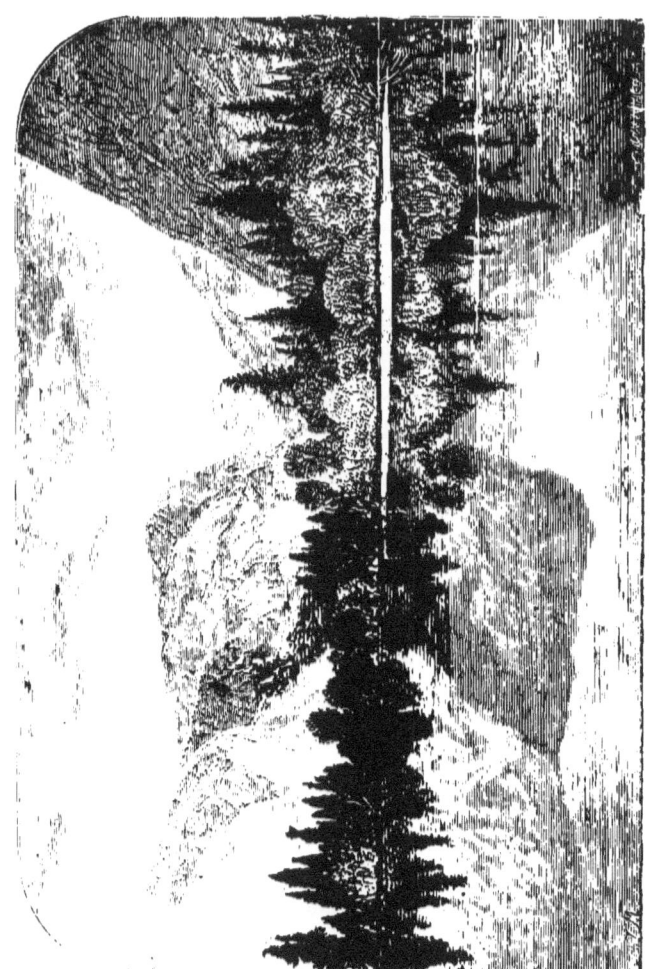

SCENE ON THUNDER BAY, LAKE SUPERIOR.

THE SEA-GULL.

THE LEGEND OF THE PICTURED ROCKS OF LAKE SUPERIOR.   OJIBWAY.

IN THE MEASURE OF HIAWATHA.

(The numerals, 1 2, etc., refer to Notes to Sea-Gull in Appendix.)

On the shore of Gitchee Gumee [2] —
Deep, mysterious, mighty waters
Where the mânitoes—the spirits—
Ride the storms and speak in thunder,
In the days of Neme-Shómis, [3]
In the days that are forgotten,
Dwelt a tall and tawny hunter—
Gitchee Péz-ze-u—the panther,
Son of Waub-Ojeeg, [4] the warrior,
Famous Waub-Ojeeg, the warrior.
Strong was he and fleet as roebuck,
Brave was he and very stealthy;
On the deer crept like a panther;
Grappled with Makwâ, [5] the monster,
Grappled with the bear and conquered;
Took his black claws for a necklet,
Took his black hide for a blanket.

When the Panther wed the Sea-Gull,
Young was he and very gladsome;

7

Fair was she and full of laughter;
Like the robin in the spring-time,
Sang from sunrise till the sunset;
For she loved the handsome hunter.
Deep as Gitchee Gumee's waters
Was her love—as broad and boundless;
And the wedded twain were happy—
Happy as the mated robins.

When their first-born saw the sunlight
Joyful was the heart of Panther,
Proud and joyful was the mother.
All the days were full of sunshine;
All the nights were full of star-light.
Nightly from the land of spirits
On them smiled the starry faces,--
Faces of their friends departed.
Little moccasins she made him,
Feathered cap and belt of wampum;
From the hide of fawn a blanket,
Fringed with feathers, soft as sable;
Singing at her pleasant labor,
By her side the tekenâgun, "
And the little hunter in it.
Oft the Panther smiled and fondled,
Smiled upon the babe and mother,
Frolicked with the boy and fondled.
Tall he grew and like his father.
And they called the boy the Raven—
Called him Kâk-kâh-gè-- the Raven.

Happy hunter was the Panther.
From the woods he brought the pheasant,

Brought the red deer and the rabbit.
Brought the trout from Gitchee Gumee—
Brought the mallard from the marshes,—
Royal feast for boy and mother:
Brought the hides of fox and beaver,
Brought the skins of mink and otter,
Lured the loon and took his blanket,
Took his blanket for the Raven.

Winter swiftly followed winter,
And again the tekenâgun
Held a babe—a tawny daughter,
Held a dark - eyed, dimpled daughter;
And they called her Waub-omeé-meé,—
Thus they named her—the White-Pigeon.
But as winter followed winter
Cold and sullen grew the Panther;
Sat and smoked his pipe in silence;
When he spoke he spoke in anger;
In the forest often tarried
Many days, and homeward turning,
Brought no game unto his wigwam:
Only brought his empty quiver,
Brought his dark and sullen visage.

Sad at heart and very lonely
Sat the Sea-Gull in the wigwam;
Sat and swung the tekenâgun,
Sat and sang to Waub-omeé-meé:
Thus she sang to Waub-omeé-meé,
Thus the lullaby she chanted:

Wâ-wa, wâ-wa, wâ-we-yeà;
Kah-wéen, nee-zhéka kè-dians-âi,
Ke-gâh nau-wâi, ne-mé-go s'wéen,
Ne-bâun, ne-bâun, ne-dâun-is-âis,
Wâ-wa, wâ-wa, wâ-we-yeà;
Ne-bâun, ne-bâun ne-dâun-is-âis,
E-we wâ-wa, wâ-we-yeà,
E-we wâ-wa, wâ-we-yeà.

[TRANSLATION.]

Swing, swing, little one, lullaby;
Thou'rt not left alone to weep;
Mother cares for you.—she is nigh;
Sleep, my little one. sweetly sleep;
Swing, swing, little one, lullaby;
Mother watches you,--she is nigh;
Gently, gently, wee one swing;
Gently, gently, while I sing
   E-we wâ - wa—lullaby,
   E-we wâ - wa—lullaby.

Homeward to his lodge returning
Kindly greeting found the hunter,
Fire to warm and food to nourish,
Golden trout from Gitchee Gumee,
Caught by Kâh - kâh - gè--the Raven.
With a snare he caught the rabbit—
Caught Wabóse,[7] the furry - footed,
Caught Penây,[7] the forest - drummer;
Sometimes with his bow and arrows,
Shot the red deer in the forest.
Shot the squirrel in the pine-top,
Shot Ne-kâ, the wild - goose, flying.
Proud as Waub - Ojeeg, the warrior,

To the lodge he bore his trophies.
So when homeward turned the Panther,
Ever found he food provided,
Found the lodge - fire brightly burning,
Found the faithful Sea - Gull waiting.
"You are cold," she said, "and famished;
Here are fire and food, my husband."
Not by word or look he answered;
Only ate the food provided,
Filled his pipe and pensive puffed it,
Smoked and sat in sullen silence.

Once—her dark eyes full of hunger—
Thus she spoke and thus besought him:
Tell me, O my silent Panther,
Tell me, O belovèd husband,
What has made you sad and sullen?
Have you met some evil spirit—
Met some goblin in the forest?
Has he put a spell upon you—
Filled your heart with bitter waters,
That you sit so sad and sullen,
Sit and smoke. but never answer,
Only when the storm is on you?"

Gruffly then the Panther answered:
"Brave among the brave is Panther,
Son of Waub - Ojeeg, the warrior,
And the brave are ever silent:
But a whining dog is woman,
Whining ever like a coward."

Forth into the tangled forest,
Threading through the thorny thickets,
Treading trails on marsh and meadow,
Sullen strode the moody hunter.
Saw he not the bear or beaver,
Saw he not the elk or roebuck;
From his path the red fawn scampered,
But no arrow followed after;
From his den the sly wolf listened,
But no twang of bow-string heard he.
Like one walking in his slumber,
Listless, dreaming, walked the Panther;
Surely had some witch bewitched him,
Some bad spirit of the forest.

When the Sea-Gull wed the Panther,
Fair was she and full of laughter;
Like the robin in the spring-time,
Sang from sunrise till the sunset;
But the storms of many winters
Sifted frost upon her tresses,
Seamed her tawny face with wrinkles.

Not alone the storms of winters
Seamed her tawny face with wrinkles.
Twenty winters for the Panther
Had she ruled the humble wigwam;
For her haughty lord and master
Borne the burdens on the journey,
Gathered fagots for the lodge-fire,
Tanned the skins of bear and beaver,
Tanned the hides of moose and red-deer;

Made him moccasins and leggins,
Decked his hood with quills and feathers—
Colored quills of Kaug,⁸ the thorny,
Feathers from Kenéw⁸ —the eagle.
For a warrior brave was Panther;
Often had he met the foemen,
Met the bold and fierce Dakotas;
Westward on the war-path met them;
And the scalps he won were numbered,
Numbered seven by Kenéw-feathers.
Sad at heart was Sea-Gull waiting,
Watching, waiting in the wigwam;
Not alone the storms of winters
Sifted frost upon her tresses.

Ka-be-bón-ík-ka,⁹ the mighty,
He that sends the cruel winter,
He that turned to stone the Giant.
From the distant Thunder-mountain,
Far across broad Gitchee Gumee,
Sent his warning of the winter,
Sent the white frost and Kewâydin,¹⁰
Sent the swift and hungry North-wind.
Homeward to the South the Summer
Turned and fled the naked forests.
With the Summer flew the robin,
Flew the bobolink and blue-bird.
Flock wise following chosen leaders,
Like the shaftless heads of arrows
Southward cleaving through the ether,
Soon the wild-geese followed after.

One long moon the Sea-Gull waited,
Watched and waited for her husband,
Till at last she heard his footsteps,
Heard him coming through the thicket.
Forth she went to meet her husband,
Joyful went to greet her husband.
Lo behind the haughty hunter,
Closely following in his footsteps,
Walked a young and handsome woman,
Walked the Red Fox from the island—
Gitchee Ménis—the Grand Island,—
Followed him into the wigwam,
Proudly took her seat beside him.
On the Red Fox smiled the hunter,
On the hunter smiled the woman.

Old and wrinkled was the Sea-Gull,
Good and true, but old and wrinkled.
Twenty winters for the Panther
Had she ruled the humble wigwam,
Borne the burdens on the journey,
Gathered fagots for the lodge-fire,
Tanned the skins of bear and beaver,
Tanned the hides of moose and red deer,
Made him moccasins and leggins,
Decked his hood with quills and feathers,
Colored quills of Kaug, the thorny,
Feathers from the great war-eagle;
Ever diligent and faithful,
Ever patient, ne'er complaining.
But like all brave men the Panther

Loved a young and handsome woman;
So he dallied with the danger,
Dallied with the fair Algónkin,[11]
Till a magic mead she gave him,
Brewed of buds of birch and cedar.[12]
Madly then he loved the woman;
Then she ruled him, then she held him
Tangled in her raven tresses,
Tied and tangled in her tresses.

Ah, the tall and tawny Panther!
Ah, the brave and brawny Panther!
Son of Waub - Ojeeg, the warrior!
With a slender hair she led him,
With a slender hair she drew him,
Drew him often to her wigwam;
There she bound him, there she held him
Tangled in her raven tresses,
Tied and tangled in her tresses.
Ah, the best of men are tangled—
Sometime tangled in the tresses
Of a fai and crafty woman.

So the Panther wed the Red Fox,
And she followed to his wigwam.
Young again he seemed and gladsome,
Glad as Raven when the father
Made his first bow from the elm-tree,
From the ash-tree made his arrows,
Taught him how to aim his arrows,
How to shoot Wabóse—the rabbit.

Then again the brawny hunter
Brought the black bear and the beaver,
Brought the haunch of elk and red-deer,
Brought the rabbit and the pheasant—
Choicest bits of all for Red Fox.
For her robes he brought the sable,
Brought the otter and the ermine,
Brought the black-fox tipped with silver.

But the Sea-Gull murmured never.
Not a word she spoke in anger,   .
Went about her work as ever,
Tanned the skins of bear and beaver,
Tanned the hides of moose and red deer,
Gathered fagots for the lodge-fire,
Gathered rushes from the marshes;
Deftly into mats she wove them;
Kept the lodge as bright as ever.
Only to herself she murmured,
All alone with Waub-omeé-meé,
On the tall and toppling highland,
O'er the wilderness of waters;
Murmured to the murmuring waters,
Murmured to the Nébe-nâw-baigs—
To the spirits of the waters;
On the wild waves poured her sorrow,
Save the infant on her bosom
With her dark eyes wide with wonder.
None to hear her but the spirits,
And the murmuring pines above her.
Thus she cast away her burdens,

Cast her burdens on the waters;
Thus unto the Mighty Spirit,
Made her lowly lamentation:
"Wahonówin!—Wahonówin!"[13]
Gitchee Mânito, benâ-nin!
Nah, Ba-bâ, showâin neméshin!
Wahonówin!—Wahonówin!"

Ka-be-bón-ík-ka,[9] the mighty,
He that sends the cruel winter,
From the distant Thunder - mountain,
On the shore of Gitchee Gumee—
On the rugged northern limit,
Sent his solemn, final warning,
Sent the white wolves of the Nor'land.[11]
Like the dust of stars in ether—
In the Pathway of the Spirits,[15]
Like the sparkling dust of diamonds,
Fell the frost upon the forest,
On the mountains and the meadows,
On the wilderness of woodland,
On the wilderness of waters.
All the lingering fowls departed—
All that seek the South in winter,
All but Shingebís, the diver;[16]
He defies the Winter-maker,
Sits and laughs at Winter-maker.

Ka-be-bón-ík-ka, the mighty,
From his wigwam called Kewâydin,—
From his home among the ice-bergs,
From the sea of frozen waters,

Called the swift and hungry North-wind.
Then he spread his 'mighty pinions
Over all the land and shook them.
Like the white down of Wâubése[17]
Fell the feathery snow and covered,
All the marshes and the meadows,
All the hill-tops and the highlands.
Then old Péböân [18] —the winter—
Laughed along the stormy waters,
Danced upon the windy headlands,
On the storm his white hair streaming,
And his steaming breath, ascending,
On the pine-tops and the cedars
Fell in frosty mists refulgent,
Sprinkling somber shades with silver,
Sprinkling all the woods with silver.

By the lodge-fire all the winter
Sat the Sea-Gull and the Red Fox,
Sat and kindly spoke and chatted,
Till the twain seemed friends together.
Friends they seemed in word and action,
But within the breast of either
Smouldered still the baneful embers—
Fires of jealousy and hatred,—
Like a camp-fire in the forest
Left by hunters and deserted;
Only seems a bed of ashes,
But the East-wind, Wâbun-noódin,
Scatters through the woods the ashes,
Fans to flame the sleeping embers,

And the wild-fire roars and rages,
Roars and rages through the forest.
So the baneful embers smouldered,
Smouldered in the breast of either.

From the far-off Sunny Islands,
From the pleasant land of Summer,
Where the spirits of the blessèd
Feel no more the fangs of hunger,
Or the cold breath of Kewâydin,
Came a stately youth and handsome.
Came Según,[10] the foe of Winter.
Like the rising sun his face was,
Like the shining stars his eyes were,
Light his footsteps as the Morning's,
In his hand were buds and blossoms,
On his brow a blooming garland.
Straightway to the icy wigwam
Of old Pébóân, the Winter,
Strode Según and quickly entered.
There old Pébóân sat and shivered,
Shivered o'er his dying lodge-fire.

"Ah, my son, I bid you welcome;
Sit and tell me your adventures;
I will tell you of my power;
We will pass the night together."
Thus spake Pébóân—the Winter;
Then he filled his pipe and lighted;
Then by sacred custom raised it
To the spirits in the ether;

To the spirits in the caverns .
Of the hollow earth he lowered it.
Thus he passed it to the spirits,
And the unseen spirits puffed it.
Next himself old Péböän honored;
Thrice he puffed his pipe and passed it,
Passed it to the handsome stranger.

"Lo I blow my breath," said Winter,
"And the laughing brooks are silent;
Hard as flint become the waters,
And the rabbit runs upon them."

Then Según, the fair youth, answered:
"Lo I breathe upon the hill-sides,
On the valleys and the meadows,
And behold, as if by magic—
By the magic of the Spirits,
Spring the flowers and tender grasses."

Then old Péböän replying:
"Nah!" I breathe upon the forests,
And the leaves fall sere and yellow;
Then I shake my locks and snow falls,
Covering all the naked landscape."

Then Según arose and answered:
"Nashké!"—see!—I shake my ringlets:
On the earth the warm rain falleth,
And the flowers look up like children
Glad-eyed from their mother's bosom.
Lo my voice recalls the robin,

Brings the bobolink and blue-bird,
And the woods are full of music.
With my breath I melt their fetters,
And the brooks leap laughing onward."

Then old Péböän looked upon him,
Looked and knew Según, the Summer.
From his eyes the big tears started
And his boastful tongue was silent.

Now Keezís[21]—the great life-giver,
From his wigwam in Waubú-nong[21]
Rose and wrapped his shining blanket
Round his giant form and started,
Westward started on his journey,
Striding on from hill to hill-top.
Upward then he climbed the ether
On the Bridge of Stars[22] he traveled.
Westward traveled on his journey
To the far-off Sunset Mountains—
To the gloomy land of shadows.

On the lodge-poles sang the robin.—
And the brooks began to murmur.
On the South-wind floated fragrance
Of the early buds and blossoms.
From old Péböän's eyes the tear-drops
Down his pale face ran in streamlets;
Less and less he grew in stature
Till he melted down to nothing;
And behold, from out the ashes,

From the ashes of his lodge-fire,
Sprang the Miscodeed[23] and, blushing,
Welcomed Según to the North-land.

So from Sunny Isles returning,
From the Summer-Land of spirits,
On the poles of Panther's wigwam
Sang Opeé-chee—sang the robin.
In the maples cooed the pigeons—
Cooed and wooed like silly lovers.
"Hah! hah!" laughed the crow derisive,
In the pine-top, at their folly,—
Laughed and jeered the silly lovers.
Blind with love were they, and saw not;
Deaf to all but love, and heard not;
So they cooed and wooed unheeding,
Till the gray hawk pounced upon them,
And the old crow shook with laughter.

On the tall cliff by the sea-shore
Red Fox made a swing. She fastened
Thongs of moose-hide to the pine-tree,
To the strong arm of the pine-tree.
Like a hawk, above the waters,
There she swung herself and fluttered,
Laughing at the thought of danger,
Swung and fluttered o'er the waters.
Then she bantered Sea-Gull, saying,
"See!—I swing above the billows!
Dare you swing above the billows,—
Swing like me above the billows?"

To herself said Sea-Gull—"Surely
I will dare whatever danger
Dares the Red Fox—dares my rival;
She shall never call me coward."
So she swung above the waters—
Dizzy height above the waters,
Pushed and aided by her rival,
To and fro with reckless daring,
Till the strong tree rocked and trembled,
Rocked and trembled with its burden.
As above the yawning billows
Flew the Sea-Gull like a whirlwind,
Red Fox, swifter than red lightning,
Cut the cords, and headlong downward,
Like an osprey from the ether,
Like a wild-goose pierced with arrows,
Fluttering fell the frantic woman,
Fluttering fell into the waters—
Plunged and sunk beneath the waters!
Hark!—the wailing of the West-wind!
Hark!—the wailing of the waters,
And the beating of the billows!
But no more the voice of Sea-Gull.

In the wigwam sat the Red Fox,
Hushed the wail of Waub-omeé-omeé,
Weeping for her absent mother.
With the twinkling stars the hunter
From the forest came and Raven.
"Sea-Gull wanders late," said Red Fox,
"Late she wanders by the sea-shore,
And some evil may befall her."

In the misty morning twilight
Forth went Panther and the Raven,
Searched the forest and the marshes,
Searched for leagues along the lake-shore,
Searched the islands and the highlands;
But they found no trace or tidings,
Found no track in marsh or meadow,
Found no trail in fen or forest,
On the shore-sand found no foot-prints.
Many days they sought and found not.
Then to Panther spoke the Raven:
"She is in the Land of Spirits—
Surely in the Land of Spirits.
High at midnight I beheld her—
Like a flying star beheld her—
To the waves of Gitchee Gumee,
Downward flashing through the ether.
Thus she flashed that I might see her,
See and know my mother's spirit;
Thus she pointed to the waters,
And beneath them lies her body.
In the wigwam of the spirits—
In the lodge of Nebe-nâw-baigs."[24]

Then spoke Panther to the Raven:
"On the tall cliff by the waters
Wait and watch with Waub-omeé-meé.
If the Sea-Gull hear the wailing
Of her infant she will answer."

On the tall cliff by the waters
So the Raven watched and waited;

All the day he watched and waited,
But the hungry infant slumbered,
Slumbered by the side of Raven,
Till the pines' gigantic shadows
Stretched and pointed to Waubú-nong[21] —
To the far - off land of Sunrise;
Then the wee one woke and famished,
Made a long and piteous wailing.

From afar where sky and waters
Meet in misty haze and mingle,
Straight toward the rocky highland,
Straight as flies the feathered arrow,
Straight to Raven and the infant
Swiftly flew a snow-white sea-gull, —
Flew and touched the earth a woman.
And behold, the long-lost mother
Caught her wailing child and nursed her,
Sang a lullaby and nursed her.

Thrice was wound a chain of silver
Round her waist and strongly fastened.
Far away into the waters —
To the wigwam of the spirits, —
To the lodge of Ne-be-nâw-baigs, —
Stretched the magic chain of silver.

Spoke the mother to the Raven:
"O my son, — my brave young hunter,
Feed my tender little orphan:
Be a father to my orphan;
Be a mother to my orphan, —

For the crafty Red Fox robbed us,—
Robbed the Sea-Gull of her husband,
Robbed the infant of her mother.
From this cliff the treacherous woman
Headlong into Gitchee Gumee
Plunged the mother of my orphan.
Then a Nebe-nâw-baig caught me,—
Chief of all the Nebe-nâw-baigs—
Took me to his shining wigwam,
In the cavern of the waters,
Deep beneath the mighty waters.
All below is burnished copper,
All above is burnished silver
Gemmed with amethyst and agates.
As his wife the Spirit holds me;
By this silver chain he holds me.

When my little one is famished,
When with long and piteous wailing
Cries the orphan for her mother,
Hither bring her, O my Raven;
I will hear her,—I will answer.
Now the Nebe-nâw-baig calls me,—
Pulls the chain,—I must obey him."

Thus she spoke and in the twinkling
Of a star the spirit-woman
Changed into a snow-white sea-gull,
Spread her wings and o'er the waters
Swiftly flew and swiftly vanished.

Then in secret to the Panther
Raven told his tale of wonder.

Sad and sullen was the hunter;
Sorrow gnawed his heart like hunger;
All the old love came upon him,
And the new love was a hatred.
Hateful to his heart was Red Fox,
But he kept from her the secret—
Kept his knowledge of the murder.
Vain was she and very haughty—
Oge-mâ-kwa[25] of the wigwam.
All in vain her fond caresses
On the Panther now she lavished;
When she smiled his face was sullen,
When she laughed he frowned upon her:
In her net of raven tresses
Now no more she held him tangled.
Now through all her fair disguises
Panther saw an evil spirit,
Saw the false heart of the woman.

On the tall cliff o'er the waters
Raven sat with Waub-omeé-meé,
Sat and watched again and waited,
Till the wee one faint and famished,
Made a long and piteous wailing.
Then again the snow-white Sea-Gull,
From afar where sky and waters
Meet in misty haze and mingle,
Straight toward the rocky highland,
Straight as flies the feathered arrow,
Straight to Raven and the infant,
With the silver chain around her,

Flew and touched the earth a woman.
In her arms she caught her infant—
Caught the wailing Waub-omeé-meé,
Sang a lullaby and nursed her.

Sprang the Panther from the thicket—
Sprang and broke the chain of silver!
With his tomahawk he broke it.
Thus he freed the willing Sea-Gull—
From the Water - Spirit freed her,
From the Chief of Nebe-nâw-baigs.

Very angry was the Spirit;
When he drew the chain of silver.
Drew and found that it was broken.
Found that he had lost the woman,
Very angry was the Spirit.
Then he raged beneath the waters,
Raged and smote the mighty waters.
Till the big sea boiled and bubbled,
Till the white-haired, bounding billows
Roared around the rocky head-lands,
Roared and plashed upon the shingle.

To the wigwam happy Panther,
As when first he wooed and won her,
Led his wife—as young and handsome.
For the waves of Gitchee Gumee
Washed away the frost and wrinkles.
And the Spirits by their magic
Made her young and fair forever.

In the wigwam sat the Red Fox,
Sat and sang a song of triumph,
For she little dreamed of danger,
Till the haughty hunter entered,
Followed by the happy mother,
Holding in her arms her infant.
When the Red Fox saw the Sea-Gull—
Saw the dead a living woman,
One wild cry she gave despairing,
One wild cry as of a demon.
Up she sprang and from the wigwam
To the tall cliff flew in terror;
Frantic sprang upon the margin,
Frantic plunged into the waters,
Headlong plunged into the waters.

Dead she tossed upon the billows:
For the Nebe-nâw-baigs knew her,
Knew the crafty, wicked woman,
And they cast her from the waters,
Spurned her from their shining wigwams;
Far away upon the shingle
With the roaring waves they cast her.
There upon her bloated body
Fed the cawing crows and ravens,
Fed the hungry wolves and foxes.

On the shore of Gitchee Gumee,
Ever young and ever handsome,
Long and happy lived the Sea-Gull,
Long and happy with the Panther.

Evermore the happy hunter
Loved the mother of his children.
Like a red star many winters
Blazed their lodge-fire on the sea-shore.
O'er the Bridge of Souls[26] together
Walked the Sea-Gull and the Panther.
To the far-off Sunny Islands—
To the Summer-Land of Spirits,
Where no more the happy hunter
Feels the fangs of frost or famine,
Or the keen blasts of Kewâydin,
Where no pain or sorrow enters,
And no crafty, wicked woman,
Sea-Gull journeyed with her husband.
There she rules his lodge forever,
And the twain are very happy,
On the far-off Sunny Islands,
In the Summer-Land of Spirits.

On the rocks of Gitchee Gumee—
On the Pictured Rocks—the Legend
Long ago was traced and written,
Pictured by the Water-Spirits;
But the storms of many winters
Have bedimmed the pictured story,
So that none can read the legend
But the Jossakeeds,[27] the prophets.

CRYSTAL BAY, LAKE MINNETONKA.

MINNETONKA.*

I sit once more on breezy shore, at sunset in this glorious June.
I hear the dip of gleaming oar. I list the singers' merry tune.
Beneath my feet the waters beat, and ripple on the polished stones.
The squirrel chatters from his seat ; the bag-pipe beetle hums and drones.

*The Dakota name for this beautiful lake is *Me-ne-a-tan-ka*—Broad Water. By dropping the "a" before "tánka" we have changed the name to *Big Water*.

The pink and gold in blooming wold,—the green hills mirrored in the lake!
The deep, blue waters, zephyr-rolled, along the murmuring pebbles break.
The maples screen the ferns, and lean the leafy lindens o'er the deep;
The sapphire, set in emerald green, lies like an Orient gem asleep.
The crimsoned west glows like the breast of *Rhuddin** when he pipes in May,
As downward droops the sun to rest, and shadows gather on the bay.
In amber sky the swallows fly, and sail and circle o'er the deep;
The light-winged night-hawks whir and cry; the silver pike and salmon leap.
The rising moon, the woods aboon, looks laughing down on lake and lea;
Weird o'er the waters shrills the loon; the high stars twinkle in the sea.
From bank and hill the whippowil sends piping forth his flute-like notes.
And clear and shrill the answers trill from leafy isles and silver throats.
The twinkling light on cape and height; the hum of voices on the shores;
The merry laughter on the night; the dip and plash of frolic oars.—
These tell the tale. On hill and dale the cities pour their gay and fair;
Along the sapphire lake they sail, and quaff like wine the balmy air.

'Tis well. Of yore from isle and shore the smoke of Indian teepees† rose;
The hunter plied the silent oar; the forest lay in still repose.
The moon-faced maid, in leafy glade, her warrior waited from the chase;
The nut-brown, naked children played, and chased the gopher on the grass.
The dappled fawn, on wooded lawn, peeped out upon the birch canoe,
Swift-gliding in the gray of dawn along the silent waters blue.
In yonder tree the great *Wanm-dee*‡ securely built her spacious nest:
The blast that swept the land-locked sea§ but rocked her clamorous
　　babes to rest.
By grassy mere the elk and deer gazed on the hunter as he came;
Nor fled with fear from bow or spear;—"so wild were they that they were
　　tame."

---

*The Welsh name for the robin.　§Lake Superior.
†Lodges.　‡Wanm-dee—the war-eagle of the Dakotas.

Ah, birch canoe, and hunter, too, have long forsaken lake and shore :
He bade his fathers' bones adieu and turned away forevermore.
But still, methinks, on dusky brinks the spirit of the warrior moves;
At crystal springs the hunter drinks, and nightly haunts the spot he loves.
For oft at night I see the light of lodge-fires on the shadowy shores,
And hear the wail some maiden's sprite above her slaughtered warrior pours.
I hear the sob, on Spirit Knob.* of Indian mother o'er her child;
And on the midnight waters throb her low *yun-he-he's*† weird and wild.
And sometimes, too, the light canoe glides like a shadow o'er the deep
At midnight, when the moon is low, and all the shores are hushed in sleep.

Alas,—Alas!—for all things pass; and we shall vanish, too, as they;
We build our monuments of brass, and granite, but they waste away.

---

*Spirit-knob is a small hill upon a point in the lake in full view from Wayzata. The spirit of a Dakota mother, whose only child was drowned in the lake during a storm, many, many years ago, often wails at midnight (so the Dakotas say), on this hill. So they called it *Wa-na-gee Pa-zo-dan*—Spirit-Knob. (Literally—little hill of the spirit.)

†Pronounced *Yoon-hay-hay*—the exclamation used by Dakota women in their lament for the dead, and equivalent to "woe-is-me."

NOTES.

---

1 Called in the Dakota tongue "Hok-sée-win-nâ-pee Wo-hàn-pee"—Virgins' Dance (or Feast).

2 One of the favorite and most exciting games of the Dakotas is ball-playing. A smooth place on the prairie, or in winter, on a frozen lake or river, is chosen. Each player has a sort of bat, called "Tâ-kée-cha-psé-cha," about thirty-two inches long with a hoop at the lower end four or five inches in diameter, interlaced with thongs of deer-skin, forming a sort of pocket. With these bats they catch and throw the ball. Stakes are set as bounds at a considerable distance from the centre on either side. Two parties are then formed, and each chooses a leader or chief. The ball (Tâ-pa) is then thrown up half way between the bounds and the game begins, the contestants contending with their bats for the ball as it falls. When one succeeds in getting it fairly in the pocket of his bat he swings it aloft and throws it as far as he can towards the bound to which his party is working, taking care to send it, if possible, where some of his own side will take it up. Thus the ball is thrown and contended for till one party succeeds in casting it beyond the bound of the opposite party. A hundred players on a side are sometimes engaged in this exciting game. Betting on the result often runs high. Moccasins, pipes, knives, hatchets, blankets, robes and guns are hung on the prize-pole. Not unfrequently horses are staked on the issue, and sometimes even women. Old men and mothers are among the spectators praising their swift-footed sons, and young wives and maidens are there to stimulate their husbands and lovers. This game is not confined to the warriors, but is also a favorite amusement of the Dakota maidens who generally play for prizes offered by the chief or warriors. (See Neill's Hist. Minn., pp 74-5; Riggs' "Tâkoo Wakân," pp 44-5, and Mrs. Eastman's Dacotah, p 55.

3 Pronounced Wah-zeé-yah. The god of the North, or Winter. A fabled spirit who dwells in the frozen North, in a great teepee of ice and snow. From his mouth and nostrils he blows the cold blasts of winter. He and "I-tó-ka-ga Wi-câs-ta"—the spirit or god of the South (literally the "South Man"), are inveterate enemies, and always on the war-path against each other. In winter Wa-zí-ya advances southward and drives "I-tó-ka-ga Wi-câs-ta" before him to the Summer-Islands. But in Spring the god of the South, having renewed his youth and strength, in the "Happy Hunting Grounds," is able to drive Wa-zí-ya back again to his icy wigwam in the North. Some Dakotas say that the numerous granite boulders, scattered over the prairies of Minnesota and Dakota, were hurled in battle by Wa-zí-ya from his home in the North at "I-tó-ka-ga Wi-câs-ta." The Wa-zí-ya of the Dakotas is substantially the same as "*Ka-be-bon-ik-ka*"—the "Winter-maker" of the Ojibways.

4 Mendota—(meeting of the waters) at the confluence of the Mississippi and Minnesota rivers. See view of the valley—front cut. The true Dakota word is Mdó-tè—applied to the mouth of a river flowing into another,—also to the outlet of a lake.

5 Pronounced Wee-wâh-stay; literally—a beautiful virgin, or woman.

6 Cetân-wa-ká-wa-mâni—"He who shoots pigeon-hawks walking"—was the full Dakota name of the grandfather of the celebrated "Little Crow" (Ta-ó-ya-te-dú-ta.—His Red People) who led his warriors in the terrible outbreak in Minnesota in 1862—3. The Chippewas called the grandfather "Kâ-kâ-keé"--crow or raven—from his war-badge, a crow-skin ; and hence the French traders and *courriers du bois* called him "*Petit Corbeau*" —Little Crow. This sobriquet, of which he was proud, descended to his son, Wakínyan Tânka—Big Thunder, who succeeded him as chief; and from Big Thunder to his son Ta-ó-ya-te-dú-ta, who became chief on the death of Wakínyan Tânka. These several "Little Crows" were successively Chiefs of the Light-foot, or Kapóza band of Dakotas. Kapóza, the principal village of this band, was originally located on the east bank of the Mississippi near the site of the city of St. Paul. Col. Minn. Hist. Soc., 1864, p. 29. It was in later years moved to the west bank. The grandfather, whom I, for short, call Wakâwa, died the death of a brave in battle against the Ojibways (commonly called Chippewas)—the hereditary enemies of the

Dakotas. Wakínyan Tânka,—Big Thunder, was killed by the accidental discharge of his own gun. They were both buried with their kindred near the "Wakan Teepee," the sacred Cave—(Carver's Cave). Ta-ó-ya-te-dú-ta, the last of the Little Crows, was killed July 3, 1863, near Hutchinson, Minnesota, by one Lamson, and his bones were duly "done up" for the Historical Society of Minnesota. For a part of the foregoing information I am indebted to Gen. H. H. Sibley. See Heard's Hist. Sioux War, and Neill's Hist. Minnesota, Third Edition.

7 Hârps-te-nâh. The first-born *daughter* of a Dakota is called Winona; the second, Hârpen; the third, Hârpstinâ; the fourth, Wâska; the fifth, Wehârka. The first born *son* is called Chaskè: the second, Hârpam; the third, Hapéda; the fourth, Châtun; the fifth, Hârka. They retain these names till others are given them on account of some action, peculiarity, etc. The females often retain their child-names through life.

8 Wah-pah-sâh was the hereditary name of a long and illustrious line of Dakota Chiefs. Wabashaw is a corrupt pronounciation. The name is a contraction of "Wâ-pa-hâ-sa," which is from "Wâ-ha-pa," the standard or pole used in the Dakota dances, and upon which feathers of various colors are tied, and not from "Wâ-pa"—leaf or leaves, as has been generally supposed. Therefore Wâpasa means the Standard—and not the "Leaf-Shaker," as many writers have it. The principal village of these hereditary Chiefs was Ke-úk-sa, or Ke-ó-sa,—where now stands the fair city of Winona. Ke-úk-sa signifies—The village of law-breakers; so-called because this band broke the law or custom of the Dakotas against marrying blood relatives of any degree. I get this information from Rev. Stephen R. Riggs, author of the Dakota Grammar and Dictionary, "*Takoo Wakan,*" etc. Wapasa, grandfather of the last Chief of that name, and a contemporary of Cetan-Wa-kâ-wa-mâni, was a noted Chief, and a friend of the British in the war of the Revolution. Neill's Hist. Minn., pp. 225—9.

9 E-hó, E-tó—Exclamations of surprise and delight.

10 Mah-gâh—The wild-goose.

11 Tce-peé—A lodge or wigwam, often contracted to "tee."

12 Pronounced Mahr-peé-yah-doó-tah—literally, Cloud Red.

13 Pronounced Wahnmdeé—The War-Eagle. Each feather worn by a warrior represents an enemy slain or captured—man, woman or child; but

the Dakotas, before they became desperate under the cruel warfare of their enemies, generally spared the lives of their captives, and never killed women or infants, except in rare instances, under the *lex talionis.* Neill's Hist. Minn., p. 112.

14 Mah-tó—The polar bear—*ursus maritimus.* The Dakotas say that, in olden times, white bears were often found about Rainy Lake and the Lake of the Woods, in winter, and sometimes as far south as the mouth of the Minnesota. They say one was once killed at White Bear Lake (but a few miles from St. Paul and Minneapolis), and they therefore named the lake Medé Mató—White Bear Lake.

15 The Hó-hé (Hó-hây) are the Assiniboins or "Stone-roasters." Their home is the region of the Assiniboin river in British America. They speak the Dakota tongue, and originally were a band of that nation. Tradition says a Dakota "Helen" was the cause of the separation and a bloody feud that lasted for many years. The Hohés are called "Stone roasters," because, until recently at least, they used "Wa-ta-pe" kettles and vessels made of birch bark in which they cooked their food. They boiled water in these vessels by heating stones and putting them in the water. The "wa-ta-pe" kettle is made of the fibrous roots of the white cedar, interlaced and tightly woven. When the vessel is soaked it becomes watertight. [Snelling's] Tales of the North west, p 21, Mackenzie's Travels.

16 Hey-ó-ka is one of the principal Dakota deities. He is a Giant, but can change himself into a buffalo, a bear, a fish or a bird. He is called the Anti-natural God or Spirit. In summer he shivers with cold, in winter he suffers from heat; he cries when he laughs and he laughs when he cries, &c. He is the reverse of nature in all things. Heyóka is universally feared and reverenced by the Dakotas, but so severe is the ordeal that the Heyóka Wacípee (the dance to Heyóka) is now rarely celebrated. It is said that the "Medicine-men" use a secret preparation which enables them to handle fire and dip their hands in boiling water without injury, and thereby gain great *eclat* from the uninitiated. The chiefs and the leading warriors usually belong to the secret order of "Medicine-men," or "Sons of Unktéhee"—the Spirit of the Waters.

17 The Dakota name for the moon is Han-yé-tu-wee—literally. Night-Sun. He is the twin brother of An-pé-tu-wee—the Day-Sun. See note 70.

18 The Dakotas believe that the stars are the spirits of their departed friends.

19 Tee--Contracted from teepee, lodge or wigwam, and means the same.

20 For all their sacred feasts the Dakotas kindle a new fire called "The Virgin Fire." This is done with flint and steel, or by rubbing together pieces of wood till friction produces fire. It must be done by a virgin, nor must any woman, except a virgin, ever touch the "sacred armor" of a Dakota warrior. White cedar is "Wakân"—sacred. See note 50. Riggs' "Tahkoo Wakân," p. 84.

21 All Northern Indians consider the East a mysterious and sacred land whence comes the sun. The Dakota name for the East is Wee-yo-heé-yan-pa —the sunrise. The Ojibways call it Waub-ó-nong—the white land or land of light, and they have many myths, legends and traditions relating thereto. Barbarous peoples of all times have regarded the East with superstitious reverence, simply because the sun rises in that quarter.

22 See Mrs. Eastman's Dacotah, pp. 225–8, describing the feast to Heyóka.

23 This stone from which the Dakotas have made their pipes for ages, is esteemed "wakân"—sacred. They call it I-yân-ska, probably from "Iya," to speak, and "ska," white, truthful, peaceful,—hence, peace-pipe, herald of peace, pledge of truth, etc. In the cabinet at Albany, N. Y., there is a very ancient pipe of this material which the Iroquois obtained from the Dakotas. Charlevoix speaks of this pipe-stone in his History of New France. LeSueur refers to the Yanktons as the village of the Dakotas at the Red-Stone Quarry. See Neill's Hist. Minn., p. 514.

24 "Ho" is an exclamation of approval—yea, yes, bravo.

25 Buying is the honorable way of taking a wife among the Dakotas. The proposed husband usually gives a horse or its value in other articles to the father or natural guardian of the woman selected—sometimes against her will. See note 75.

26 The Dakotas believe that the *Aurora Borealis* is an evil omen and the threatening of an evil spirit, (perhaps Wazíya, the Winter-god—some say a witch, or a very ugly old woman). When the lights appear, danger threatens, and the warriors shoot at, and often slay, the evil spirit, but it rises from the dead again.

27 Se-só-kah—The Robin.

28 The spirit of Anpétu-sâpa that haunts the Falls of St. Anthony with
her dead babe in her arms. See the Legend in Neill's Hist. Minn., or my
"Legend of the Falls."

29 Mee-coónk-shee—My daughter.

30 The Dakotas call the meteor, "Wakân-denda" (sacred fire) and
Wakân-wohlpa (sacred gift.) Meteors are messengers from the Land of
Spirits, warning of impending danger. It is a curious fact that the "sacred
stone" of the Mohammedans, in the Kaaba at Mecca, is a meteoric stone,
and obtains its sacred character from the fact that it fell from heaven.

31 Kah-nó-te-dahn—The little, mysterious dweller in the woods. This
spirit lives in the forest in hollow trees. Mrs. Eastman's Dacotah, Pre.
Rem. xxxi. "The Dakota god of the woods—an unknown animal said to
resemble a man, which the Dakotas worship: perhaps, the monkey."
Riggs' Dakota Dic. Tit—*Canotidan.*

32 The Dakotas believe that thunder is produced by the flapping of the
wings of an immense bird which they call Wakínyan—the Thunder-bird.
Near the source of the Minnesota River is a place called "Thunder-Tracks"
where the foot-prints of a "Thunder-bird" are seen on the rocks twenty-five
miles apart. Mrs. Eastman's Dacotah, p. 71. There are many Thunder-
birds. The father of all the Thunder-birds—"Wakínyan Tanka"—or "Big
Thunder," has his teepee on a lofty mountain in the far West. His teepee
has four openings, at each of which is a sentinel; at the east, a butterfly;
at the west, a bear; at the south, a red deer; at the north, a caribou. He
has a bitter enmity against Unktéhee (god of waters) and often shoots his
fiery arrows at him, and hits the earth, trees, rocks, and sometimes men.
Wakínyan created wild-rice, the bow and arrow, the tomahawk and the
spear. He is a great war-spirit, and Wanmdée (the war-eagle) is his mes-
senger. A Thunder-bird (say the Dakotas) was once killed near Kapóza
by the son of Cetan-Wakawa-mâni, and he there upon took the name of
"Wakínyan Tanka"-"Big Thunder."

33 Pronounced Tah-tâhn-kah—Bison or Buffalo.

34 Enâh—An exclamation of wonder. Ehó—Behold! see there!

35 The Crees are the Knisteneaux of Alexander Mackenzie. See his account of them, Mackenzie's Travels, (London 1801) p. xci to cvii.

9

36 Lake Superior. The only names the Dakotas have for Lake Superior are Medé Tânka or Tânka Medé - Great Lake, and Me-ne-yá-ta—literally, *At-the-Water.*

37 April—Literally, the moon when the geese lay eggs. See note 71.

38 Carver's Cave at St. Paul was called by the Dakotas "Wakân Teepee"—sacred lodge. In the days that are no more, they lighted their Council-fires in this cave, and buried their dead near it. See Neill's Hist. Minn., p. 207. Capt. Carver in his *Travels*, London, 1778, p. 63, et. seq., describes this cave as follows: "It is a remarkable cave of an amazing depth. The Indians term it Wakon-teebe, that is, the Dwelling of the Great Spirit. The entrance into it is about ten feet wide, the height of it five feet, the arch within is near fifteen feet high and about thirty feet broad. The bottom of it consists of fine clear sand. About twenty feet from the entrance begins a lake, the water of which is transparent, and extends to an unsearchable distance; for the darkness of the cave prevents all attempts to acquire a knowledge of it. I threw a small pebble towards the interior parts of it with my utmost strength. I could hear that it fell into the water, and notwithstanding it was of so small a size, it caused an astonishing and horrible noise that reverberated through all those gloomy regions. I found in this cave many Indian hieroglyphics, which appeared very ancient, for time had nearly covered them with moss, so that it was with difficulty I could trace them. They were cut in a rude manner upon the inside of the walls, which were composed of a stone so extremely soft that it might be easily penetrated with a knife: a stone everywhere to be found near the Mississippi. This cave is only accessible by ascending a narrow, steep passage that lies near the brink of the river. At a little distance from this dreary cavern is the burying-place of several bands of the Naudowessie (Dakota) Indians." Many years ago the roof fell in, but the cave has been partially restored and is now used as a beer cellar.

39 Wah-kahn-dee—The lightning.

40 The Bloody River—the Red River was so-called on account of the numerous Indian battles that have been fought on its banks. The Chippewas say that its waters were colored red by the blood of many warriors slain on its banks in the fierce wars between themselves and the Dakotas.

41 Tah—The Moose. This is the root-word for all ruminating animals;

Ta-tânka, buffalo—Ta-tóka, mountain antelope—Ta-hinca, the red-deer— Ta-mdóka, the buck-deer—Ta-hinca-ska, white-deer (sheep).

42 Hogâhn—Fish. Red Hogan, the trout.

43 Tipsânna (often called *tipsinna*), is a wild prairie-turnip used for food by the Dakotas. It grows on high, dry land, and increases from year to year. It is eaten both cooked and raw.

44 Rio Tajo, (or Tagus), a river of Spain and Portugal.

45   * * * *   "Bees of Trebizond—
Which from the sunniest flowers that glad
With their pure smile the gardens round,
Draw venom forth that drives men mad."
— *Thomas Moore.*

46 Skeé-skah—The Wood-duck.

47 The Crocus. I have seen the prairies in Minnesota spangled with these beautiful flowers in various colors before the ground was entirely free from frost. The Dacotas call them frost-flowers.

48 The "Sacred Ring" around the feast of the Virgins is formed by armed warriors sitting, and none but a virgin must enter this ring. The warrior who knows is bound on honor, and by old and sacred custom, to expose and publicly denounce any tarnished maiden who dares to enter this ring, and his word can not be questioned—even by the chief. See Mrs. Eastman's Dacotah, p. 64.

49 Prairie's Pride.—This annual shrub, which abounds on many of the sandy prairies in Minnesota, is sometimes called "tea-plant," "sage-plant," and "red-root willow." I doubt if it has any botanic name. Its long plumes of purple and gold are truly the "pride of the prairies."

50 The Dakotas consider white cedar "Wakân," (sacred). They use sprigs of it at their feasts, and often burn it to destroy the power of evil spirits. Mrs. Eastman's Dacotah, p. 210.

51 Tâhkoo-skahng-skahng.—This deity is supposed to be invisible, yet everywhere present; he is an avenger and a searcher of hearts. (Neill's Hist. Minn., p. 57.) I suspect he was the chief spirit of the Dakotas before the missionaries imported "Wakan Tânka"—(Great Spirit).

52 The Dakotas believe in "were-wolves" as firmly as did our Saxon

ancestors and for similar reasons—the howl of the wolf being often imitated as a decoy or signal by their enemies, the Ojibways.

53 Shee-shó-kah—The Robin.

54 The Dakotas call the Evening Star the "*Virgin Star*," and believe it to be the spirit of the virgin wronged at the feast.

55 Mille Lacs. This lake was discovered by DuLuth, and by him named Lac Buade, in honor of Governor Frontenac of Canada, whose family name was Buade. The Dakota name for it is Mdé Wakân—Spirit Lake.

56 The Ojibways imitate the hoot of the owl and the howl of the wolf to perfection, and often use these cries as signals to each other in war and the chase.

57 The Dakotas called the Ojibways the "Snakes of the Forest," on account of their lying in ambush for their enemies.

58 Strawberries. 59 Seé-yo—The Prairie-hen.

60 Mahgâh—The Wild-goose. *Fox-pups.* I could never see the propriety of calling the young of foxes *kits* or *kittens*, which mean *little cats*. The fox belongs to the *canis*, or dog family, and not the *felis*, or cat family. If it is proper to call the young of dogs and wolves *pups*, it is equally proper to so call the young of foxes.

61 When a Dakota is sick he thinks the spirit of an enemy or some animal has entered into his body, and the principal business of the "medicineman"—*Wicasta Wakan*—is to cast out the "unclean spirit," with incantations and charms. See Neill's Hist. Minn., pp. 66—8. The Jews entertained a similar belief in the days of Jesus of Nazareth.

62 Wah-zeé-yah's star—The North-star. See note 3.

63 The Dakotas, like our forefathers and all other barbarians, believe in witches and witchcraft.

64 The Medó is a wild potato; it resembles the sweet-potato in top and taste. It grows in bottom-lands, and is much prized by the Dakotas for food. The "Dakota Friend," for December. 1850.

65 The meteor—Wakân-denda—Sacred fire.

66 Meetâhwin—My bride.

67 Stoke—The body of a tree. This is an old English word of Saxon origin, now changed to *stock*.

68 The *Via Lactea* or Milky Way. The Dakotas call it *Wanagee-Tach-anku*—The path-way of the spirits; and believe that over this path the spirits of the dead pass to the Spirit-land. See Riggs' Tah-koo Wah-kan, p. 101.

69 Oon-Ktay-he. There are many Unktéhees, children of the Great Unktéhee, who created the earth and man, and who formerly dwelt in a vast cavern under the Falls of St. Anthony. The Unktéhee sometimes reveals himself in the form of a huge buffalo-bull. From him proceed invisible influences. The Great Unktéhee created the earth. "Assembling in grand conclave all the aquatic tribes he ordered them to bring up dirt from beneath the waters, and proclaimed death to the disobedient. The beaver and otter forfeited their lives. At last the muskrat went beneath the waters, and, after a long time, appeared at the surface, nearly exhausted, with some dirt. From this, Unktéhee fashioned the earth into a large circular plain. The earth being finished, he took a deity, one of his own offspring, and grinding him to powder, sprinkled it upon the earth, and this produced many worms. The worms were then collected and scattered again. They matured into infants and these were then collected and scattered and became full-grown Dakotas. The bones of the mastodon, the Dakotas think are the bones of Unktéhees, and they preserve them with the greatest care in the medicine bag." Neill's Hist. Minn., p. 55. The Unktéhees and the Thunder-birds are perpetually at war. There are various accounts of the creation of man. Some say that at the bidding of the Great Unktéhee, men sprang full grown from the caverns of the earth. See Riggs' "Tah-koo Wahkân, and Mrs. Eastman's Dacotah. The Great Unktéhee and the Great Thunder-bird had a terrible battle in the bowels of the earth to determine which should be the ruler of the world. See description in Legend of Winona.

70 Pronounced Ahng-pay-too-wee—The Sun; literally the Day-Sun, thus distinguishing him from Han-yé-tuwee (Hahng-yay-too-wee) the night sun, (the moon). They are twin brothers, but Anpétuwee is the more powerful. Han-yé-tuwee receives his power from his brother and obeys him. He watches over the earth while the sun sleeps. The Dakotas believe the sun is the father of life. Unlike the most of their other gods, he is beneficent and kind; yet they worship him (in the sun-dance) in the most dreadful manner. See Riggs' "Takhoo Wakan," pp. 81-2, and Catlin's "Okee-

pa." The moon is worshipped as the representative of the sun; and in the great Sun-dance, which is usually held in the full of the moon, when the moon rises the dancers turn their eyes on her (or him). Anpétuwee issues every morning from the lodge of Han-nan-na (the Morning) and begins his journey over the sky to his lodge in the land of shadows. Sometimes he walks over on the Bridge (or path) of the Spirits—Wanâgee Ta-chan-ku,— and sometimes he sails over the sea of the skies in his shining canoe; but *somehow*, and the Dakotas do not explain how, he gets back again to the lodge of Hannanna in time to take a nap and eat his breakfast before starting anew on his journey. The Dakotas swear by the sun, "*As Anpe-tu-wee hears me, this is true!*" They call him Father and pray to him —"*Wakan! Ate, on-she-ma-da.*" "Sacred Spirit,—Father, have mercy on me." As the Sun is the father, so they believe the Earth is the mother, of life. Truly there is much philosophy in the Dakota mythology. The Algonkins call the earth "*Me-suk-kum-mik-o-kwa*"—the great grandmother of all. Narrative of John Tanner, p. 193.

71 The Dakotas reckon their months by *moons.* They name their moons from natural circumstances. They correspond very nearly with our months, as follows:

January—Wee-té-rhee—The Hard Moon, i. e—the cold moon.

February—Wee-câ-ta-wee—The Coon Moon.

March—Istâ-wee-ca-ya-zang-wee—the sore-eyes moon (from snow blindness.)

April—Magâ-okâ-da-wee—the moon when the geese lay eggs; also called Wokâda-wee—egg-moon, and sometimes Watô-papee-wee, the canoe-moon, or moon when the streams become free from ice.

May—Wó-zu-pee-wee—the planting moon.

June—Wazú-ste-ca-sa-wee—the strawberry moon.

July—Wa-sun-pa-wee—moon when the geese shed their feathers, also called Chang-pâ-sapa-wee—Choke-Cherry moon, and sometimes—Mna-rchâ-rcha-wee—"The moon of the red-blooming lilies," literally, the red-lily moon.

August—Wasú-ton-wee—the ripe moon i. e. Harvest Moon.

September—Psin-na-ké-tu-wee—the ripe-rice moon.

October—Wâ-zu-pee-wee or Wee-w-azu-pee—the moon when wild-rice is gathered and laid up for winter.

November—Ta-kee-yu-hrâ-wee—the deer-rutting moon.

December—Ta-hé-cha-psing-wee—the moon when deer shed their horns.

72 Oonk-tó-mee—is a "bad spirit" in the form of a monstrous black spider. He inhabits fens and marshes and lies in wait for his prey. At night he often lights a torch (evidently the *ignis fatuus* or Jack-a-lantern) and swings it on the marshes to decoy the unwary into his toils.

73 The Dakotas have their stone-idol, or god, called Toon-kan—or In-yan. This god dwells in stone or rocks and is, they say, the *oldest god of all*—he is grandfather of all living things. I think, however, that the stone is merely the symbol of the everlasting, all pervading, invisible *Ta-ku Wa-kan*—the essence of all life,—pervading all nature, animate and inanimate. The Rev. S. R. Riggs who, for forty years, has been a student of Dakota customs, superstitions, etc., says, "Tâhkoo Wahkan," p. 55, et seq. "The religious faith of the Dakota is not in his gods as such. It is in an intangible, mysterious something of which they are only the embodiment, and that in such measure and degree as may accord with the individual fancy of the worshipper. Each one will worship some of these divinities, and neglect or despise others, but the great object of all their worship, whatever its chosen medium, is the *Ta-koo Wa-kan*, which is the *supernatural* and *mysterious*. No one term can express the full meaning of the Dakota's *Wakan*. It comprehends all mystery, secret power and divinity. Awe and reverence are its due, and it is as unlimited in manifestation as it is in idea. All life is *Wakan*; so also is everything which exhibits power, whether in action, as the winds and drifting clouds; or in passive endurance, as the boulder by the wayside. For even the commonest sticks and stones have a spiritual essence which must be reverenced as a manifestation of the all-pervading, mysterious power that fills the universe."

74 Wazi-kuté—Wah-ze-koo-tay; literally—Pine-shooter,—he that shoots among the pines. When Father Hennepin was at Mille Lacs in 1679–80, Wazi-kuté was the head Chief (Itâncan) of the band of Isantees. Hennepin writes his name—Ouasicoudé and translates it—the "Pierced Pine." See Shea's Hennepin, p. 234, Minn. Hist. Coll. vol. 1, p. 316.

75 When a Dakota brave wishes to "propose" to a "dusky maid," he visits her teepee at night after she has retired, or rather, laid down in her robe to sleep. He lights a splinter of wood and holds it to her face. If

she blows out the light, he is accepted; if she covers her head and leaves
it burning, he is rejected. The rejection however is not considered final
till it has been thrice repeated. Even then the maiden is often bought of
her parents or guardian, and forced to become the wife of the rejected suitor. If she accepts the proposal, still the suitor must buy her of
her parents with suitable gifts.

76 The Dakotas called the Falls of St. Anthony the Ha-Ha—the *loud
laughing*, or *roaring*. The Mississippi River they called Ha-Ha Wâ-kpa—
River of the Falls. The Ojibway name for the Falls is Ka-kâ-bih-kúng.
Minnehaha is a combination of two Dakota words—Mini—water and Ha-
Ha · Falls; but it is not the name by which the Dakotas designated that
cataract. Some authorities say they called it ! hâ-ha—pronounced E-
rhah-rhah—lightly laughing. Rev. S. W. Pond, whose long residence as a
missionary among the Dakotas in this immediate vicinity makes him an
authority that can hardly be questioned, says they called the Falls of Minnehaha "Mini-i-hrpâ-ya-dan," and it had no other name in Dakota. It
means Little Falls and nothing else." Letter to the author.

77 The game of the Plum-stones is one of the favorite games of the Dakotas. Hennepin was the first to describe this game in his "Description
de la Louisiane," Paris, 1683, and he describes it very accurately. See
Shea's translation p. 301. The Dakotas call this game *Kan-soo Koo-tay-
pe*—shooting plum-stones. Each stone is painted black on one side and
red on the other; on one side they grave certain figures which makes the
stones "Wakan." They are placed in a dish and thrown up like dice; indeed the game is virtually a game of dice. Hennepin says: "There are
some so given to this game that they will gamble away even their great
coat. Those who conduct the game cry at the top of their voices when
they rattle the platter and they strike their shoulders so hard as to leave
them all black with the blows."

78 Wa'tanka—contraction of Wa-kan Tanka—Great Spirit. The Dakotas had no Wakan Tanka—or Wakan-péta—fire spirit—till whitemen imported them. There being no name for the Supreme Being in the Dakota tongue (except Tanka Wakan—See note 73)—and all their gods and
spirits being Wakan—the missionaries named God in Dakota—"*Wakan
Tanka*"—which means *Big Spirit*, or *The Big Mysterious*.

79 The Dakotas called Lake Calhoun—Mdé-mdó-za—Loon Lake. They also called it—*Re-ya-ta-mde*—the lake back from the river. They called Lake Harriet—Mdé-únma—the other lake—or (perhaps) Mdé úma—Hazel-nut Lake. The lake nearest Calhoun on the north—Lake of the Isles—they called Wí-ta Mdé—Island-Lake. Lake Minnetonka they called Me-me-a-tán-ka—*Broad Water*.

80 The animal called by the French *voyageurs* the *cabri* (the kid) is found only on the prairies. It is of the goat kind, smaller than a deer, and so swift that neither horse nor dog can overtake it. (Snelling's) "Tales of the Northwest," p. 286, note 15. It is the gazelle, or prairie antelope, called by the Dakotas Tato-ka-dan—little antelope. It is the *Pish-tah-te-koosh* of the Algonkin tribes, "reckoned the fleetest animal in the prairie country about the Assinneboin." Captivity and Adventures of John Tanner, p. 301.

81 The Wicâstâpi Wakânpi (literally, *men supernatural*) are the "Medicine-men" or Magicians of the Dakotas. They call themselves the sons or disciples of Unktéhee. In their rites, ceremonies, tricks and pretensions they closely resemble the Dactyli, Idæ and Curetes of the ancient Greeks and Romans, the Magi of the Persians, and the Druids of Britain. Their pretended intercourse with spirits, their powers of magic and divination, and their rites are substantially the same, and point unmistakably to a common origin. The Dakota "Medicine-Man" can do the "rope-trick" of the Hindoo magician to perfection. The teepee used for the *Wakan Wacipee*—or Sacred Dance—is called the *Wakan Teepee*—the Sacred Teepee. Carver's Cave at St. Paul was also called Wakan Teepee, because the Medicine-men or magicians often held their dances and feasts in it. For a full account of the rites, etc., see Riggs' "Tâhkoo Wahkan, Chapter VI. The *Ta-sha-ke*—literally, "Deer-hoofs"—is a rattle made by hanging the hard segments of deer-hoofs to a wooden rod a foot long—about an inch in diameter at the handle end, and tapering to a point at the other. The clashing of these horny bits makes a sharp, shrill sound something like distant sleigh-bells. In their incantations over the sick they sometimes use the gourd-shell rattle.

The Chân-che-ga—is a drum or "Wooden Kettle." The hoop of the drum is from a foot to eighteen inches in diameter, and from three to ten

9*

inches deep. The skin covering is stretched over one end, making a drum with one end only. The magical drum-sticks are ornamented with down, and heads of birds or animals are carved on them This makes them Wakan.

The flute called *Cho-tanka* (big pith) is of two varieties—one made of sumac, the pith of which is punched out, etc. The second variety is made of the long bone of the wing or thigh of the swan or crane. They call the first the *bubbling chotanka*, from the tremulous note it gives when blown with all the holes stopped. Riggs' Tahkoo Wahkan, p. 476, et seq.

E-né-pee—vapor-bath, is used as a purification preparatory to the sacred feasts. The vapor bath is taken in this way: ".A number of poles, the size of hoop-poles or less are taken, and their larger ends being set in the ground in a circle, the flexible tops are bent over and tied in the centre. This frame work is then covered with robes and blankets, a small hole being left on one side for an entrance. Before the door a fire is built, and round stones, about the size of a man's head, are heated in it. When hot, they are rolled within, and the door being closed, steam is made by pouring water on them. The devotee, stripped to the skin, sits within this steam-tight dome, sweating profusely at every pore, until he is nearly suffocated. Sometimes a number engage in it together and unite their prayers and songs.""Tâhkoo Wakan," p. 83. Father Hennepin was subjected to the vapor-bath at Mille Lacs by Chief Aqui-pa-que-tin, two hundred years ago. After describing the method, Hennepin says: "When he had made me sweat thus three times in a week, I felt as strong as ever." Shea's Hennepin, p. 228. For a very full and accurate account of the Medicine-men of the Dakotas, and their rites, etc., see Chap. II, Neill's Hist. Minnesota.

82 The sacred *O-zu-ha*—or Medicine-sack, must be made of the skin of the otter, the coon, the weazel, the squirrel, the loon, a certain kind of fish, or the skins of serpents. It must contain four kinds of medicine (or magic) representing birds, beasts, herbs and trees, viz: The down of the female swan colored red, the roots of certain grasses, bark from the roots of cedar trees, and hair of the buffalo. "From this combination proceeds a Wakân influence so powerful that no human being, unassisted, can resist it." Wonderful indeed must be the magic power of these Dakota Druids to lead such a man as the Rev. S. R. Riggs to say of them: "By great

shrewdness, untiring industry, and more or less of *actual demoniacal posses-sion*, they convince great numbers of their fellows, and in the process are convinced *themselves*, of their sacred character and office." Tahkoo Wak-ân, pp. 88—9

83 Gâh-ma-na-tek-wâhk—*the river of many falls*—is the Ojibway name of the river commonly called Kaministiguia, near the mouth of which is situate Fort William, on the site of DuLuth's old fort. The view on Thunder-Bay is one of the grandest in America. Thunder-Cap, with its sleeping stone-giant, looms up into the heavens. Here *Ka-be-bon-ikka*—the Ojibway's god of storms, flaps his huge wings and makes the Thunder. From this mountain he sends forth the rain, the snow, the hail, the lightning and the tempest. A vast giant, turned to stone by his magic, lies asleep at his feet. The island called by the Ojibways the *Mak-i-nak* (the turtle) from its tortoise-like shape, lifts his huge form in the distance. Some "down-east" Yankee, called it "Pie-Island," from its (to his hungry imagination) fancied resemblance to a pumpkin pie, and the name, like all bad names, *sticks*. McKay's Mountain on the main-land, a perpendicular rock more than a thousand feet high, up-heaved by the throes of some vast volcano, and numerous other bold and precipitous head-lands, and rock-built islands, around which roll the sapphire-blue waters of the fathomless bay, present some of the most magnificent views to be found on either continent.

84 The Mission of the Holy Ghost—at La Pointe, on the isle Waug-a-bâ-me—(winding view) in the beautiful bay of Cha-quam-egon—was founded by the Jesuits about the year 1660. and Father Renè Menard was the first priest at this point. After he was lost in the wilderness, Father Glaude Allouëz permanently established the mission in 1665. The famous Father Marquette, who took Allouëz's place, Sept. 13, 1669, writing to his Superior. thus describes the Dakotas: "The Nadouessi are the Iroquois of this country, beyond La Pointe, *but less faithless, and never attack till at-tacked*. Their language is entirely different from the Huron and Algon-quin. They have many villages, but are widely scattered. They have very extraordinary customs. They principally use the calumet. They do not speak at great feasts, and when a stranger arrives give him to eat of a wooden fork, as we would a child. All the lake tribes make war on them, but with small success. They have false oats, (wild rice) use little canoes, *and keep their word strictly*." Neill's Hist. Minn., p. 111.

85 Michâbo—the Good. Great Spirit of the Algonkins. In Autumn, in the moon of the falling leaf, ere he composes himself to his winter's sleep, he fills his great pipe and takes a god-like smoke. The balmy clouds from his pipe float over the hills and woodland, filling the air with the haze of "Indian Summer." Brinton's Myths of the New World, p. 163.

86 Pronounced *Kah-thah-gah*—literally, *the place of waves and foam.* This was the principal village of the Isantee band of Dakotas two hundred years ago, and was located at the Falls of St. Anthony, which the Dakotas called the *Ha-ha*,—pronounced *Rhah-rhah*,—the *loud, laughing waters.* The Dakotas believed that the Falls were in the centre of the earth. Here dwelt the Great Unktéhee, the creator of the earth and man; and from this place a path led to the Spirit-land. DuLuth undoubtedly visited Kathâga in the year 1679. In his "Memoir" (Archives of the Ministry of the Marine) addressed to Seignelay, 1685, he says: "On the 2nd of July, 1679, I had the honor to plant his Majesty's arms in the great village of the Nadouecioux called Izatys, where never had a Frenchman been, etc." *Izatys* is here used not as the name of the village, but as the name of the band—the Isantees. *Nadouecioux* was a name given the Dakotas generally by the early French traders and the Ojibways. See Shea's Hennepin's Description of Louisiana pp. 203 and 375. The villages of the Dakotas were not permanent towns. They were hardly more than camping grounds, occupied at intervals and for longer or shorter periods, as suited the convenience of the hunters; yet there were certain places, like Mille Lacs, the Falls of St. Anthony, Kapóza (near St. Paul), Remnica, (where the city of Red Wing now stands), and Keúxa (or Keóza) on the site of the city of Winona, so frequently occupied by several of the bands as to be considered their chief villages respectively.

NOTES TO THE SEA-GULL.

1 Kay-óshk is the Ojibway name of Sea-Gull.

2 Gitchee—great,—Gumee—sea or lake,—Lake Superior: also often called Ochípwè Gítchee Gúmee, Great Lake (or sea) of the Ojibways.

3 Né-mè-Shómis—my grandfather. "In the days of my Grandfather" is the Ojibway's preface to all his traditions and legends.

4 Waub—white,—O-jeeg,—fisher, (a furred animal.) White Fisher was the name of a noted Chippewa Chief who lived on the south shore of Lake Superior many years ago. Schoolcraft married one of his descendants.

5 Ma-kwâ or mush-kwa—the bear.

6 The Te-ke-nâh-gun is a board upon one side of which a sort of basket is fastened or woven with thongs of skin or strips of cloth. In this the babe is placed, and the mother carries it on her back. In the wigwam the teke-nagun is often suspended by a cord to the lodge-poles and the mother swings her babe in it.

7 Wabóse—the rabbit. Penay, the pheasant. At certain seasons the pheasant drums with his wings.

8 Kaug, the porcupine. Kenéw, the war-eagle.

9 Ka-be-bón-ík-ka is the god of storms, thunder, lightning, etc. His home is on Thunder-Cap at Thunder-Bay, Lake Superior. By his magic, the giant that lies on the mountain was turned to stone. He always sends warnings before he finally sends the severe cold of winter, in order to give all creatures time to prepare for it.

10 Kewaydin or Kewaytin, is the North-wind or North-west wind.

11 Algónkin is the general name applied to all tribes that speak the Ojibway language or dialects of it.

12 This is the favorite "love-broth" of the Ojibway squaws. The warrior who drinks it immediately falls desperately in love with the woman who gives it to him. Various tricks are devised to conceal the nature of the "medicine" and to induce the warrior to drink it; but when it is mixed with a liberal quantity of "fire-water" it is considered irresistable.

13 Translation: Woe-is-me! Woe-is-me!
Great Spirit, behold me!
Look, Father; have pity upon me!
Woe-is-me! Woe-is-me!

14 Snow-storms from the North-west.

15 The Ojibways, like the Dakotas, call the *Via Lactea* (Milky Way) the Pathway of the Spirits.

16 Shingebís, the diver, is the only water-fowl that remains about Lake Superior all winter. See Schoolcraft's Hiawatha Legends, p. 113.

17 Wanb-ése—the white swan.

18 Pé-böán, Winter, is represented as an old man with long white hair and beard.

19 Se-gún is Spring or Summer. This beautiful allegory has been "done into verse" by Longfellow in *Hiawatha*. I took my version from the lips of an old Chippewa Chief. I have compared it with Schoolcraft's version, from which Mr. Longfellow evidently took his.

20 Nah—look, see. Nashké—behold.

21 Kee-zis—the sun,—the father of life. Waubúnong—or Wanb-ó-nong —is the White Land or Land of Light,—the Sun-rise, the East.

22 The Bridge of Stars spans the vast sea of the skies, and the sun and moon walks over on it.

23 The Miscodeed is a small white flower with a pink border. It is the earliest blooming wild-flower on the shores of Lake Superior, and belongs to the crocus family.

24 The Ne-be-naw-baigs, are Water-spirits; they dwell in caverns in the depths of the lake, and in some respects resemble the Unktéhees of the Dakotas.

25 Ogema, Chief,—Ogema-kwa—female Chief. Among the Algonkin tribes women are sometimes made chiefs. Wet-nó-kwa, who adopted Tanner as her son, was Oge-mâ-kwa of a band of Ottawas. See John Tanner's Narrative, p. 36.

26 The "Bridge of Souls" leads from the earth over dark and stormy waters to the Spirit-land. The "Dark River" seems to have been a part of the superstition of all nations.

27 The Jossakeeds of the Ojibways are sooth-sayers who are able, by the aid of spirits, to read the past as well as the future.

APR 29 1902

ERRATA.

[Will the reader please correct the following errors of the printers. I regret to find hem so numerous. I presume there are others I have overlooked in my hasty eading.—H. L. G.]

Page 31, line 24—Read *eyes* instead of *eye*.
" 52, " 18 " "*are* fathomed" instead of *is*, *etc*.
" 62, " 26-29 " *monteds* instead of *moutcds*.
" 64, " 13 " *sip*, instead of *sipped*.
" 64, " 23 " Wa'tánka.*
" 65, " 29 " *eagle*-winged, instead of *eagled*-winged.
" 68, " 22 " *Unktehee*, instead of *Untehee*.
" 69, " 5 " "let the word of *a* warrior be sacred."
" 69, " 6 " "be he *friend* of the band or *a* foeman."
" 72, " 17 " *Niwásté*, instead of *Wiwasté*.
" 74, " 13 " "Till away in the bend of *the* stream."
" 74, " 29 " *Wakán* instead of *Wahán*.
" 81, " 23 " "*dreamy* haze," instead of "*dreary haze*."
" 86, " 20 " *Ta-té-psin*, instead of *Ma-te-psin*.
" 133, " 4 " *Oonk táy-hee* instead of *Oon-Ktay-he*.
" 134, " 35 " Wee-wa-zú-pee.
" 135, " 2 " *Ta-hé-cha-psung-wee*.
" 136, " 12 " I-ha-ha.
" 136, " 23 " "*Which make*," instead of "*which makes*."
" 136, " 33 " *Tá-ku Wakan*, instead of *Tanka Wakan*.
" 137, " 6 " Me-*ne*-a-tan-ka.
" 139, " 14 " "*its* huge form," in lieu of "*his*," etc.
" 142, " 29 " *walk* instead of *walks*.
" 143, " 5 " *Net*-no-kwa, instead of *Wet*-no-kwa.